MORE GREEK FOLKTALES

MORE GREEK FOLKTALES

CHOSEN AND TRANSLATED BY

R. M. DAWKINS

GREENWOOD PRESS, PUBLISHERS
WESTPORT, CONNECTICUT

Library of Congress Cataloging in Publication Data

Dawkins, Richard McGillivray, 1871-1955, ed. and tr.
More Greek folktales.

Reprint of the 1955 ed. published by Clarendon Press, London.
1. Tales, Greek (Modern) I. Title.
GR170.D32 1974 398.2'09495 74-9218
ISBN 0-8371-7631-X

Originally published in 1955 by the Clarendon Press, Oxford

This reprint has been authorized by the Clarendon Press Oxford

Reprinted in 1974 by Greenwood Press, a division of Williamhouse-Regency Inc.

Library of Congress Catalog Card Number 74-9218

ISBN 0-8371-7631-X

Preface

In 1953 *Modern Greek Folktales* was published, a collection of translations in which I aimed at bringing together as completely as I could all the folktales commonly traditional among the Greek people. This limitation to widely spread stories excluded those which had, as yet at all events, been recorded perhaps once only: these can, on our evidence, hardly be called a part of the body of really traditional stories. It is these stories, excluded in principle from the earlier book, that make up the bulk of this present collection. There are, however, a few exceptions. Nos. 1 and 5 have a certain dependence on stories in the earlier book, and appear here as being variants of some special interest. Of No. 9 I then gave only an outline. No. 22 is a story with many variants and ought to have appeared in the earlier book. So ought No. 3, and would have, if I had not then decided to exclude animal stories, which are, except perhaps in Pontos, not very common in Greece. The Greeks seem more interested in human beings than in the imaginary doings of animals, and here I am inclined to feel with them; yet such a widely spread genre of story-telling should not be entirely neglected.

It has not been possible to establish any strictly logical order in which to present these stories. In general I have followed the lines of the earlier book, and so I begin with two fairy stories; then I put No. 3, my one animal story. Towards the end I have put the two novels, Nos. 23 and 24, as belonging to a more developed genre, and have ended with two rather more serious stories. For those between, Nos. 4 to 22, I have tried to put the stories which largely involve the supernatural rather before those in which it plays a smaller part. Beyond this I have not been able to go.

Here is the place to express my various obligations. To the editors of *Arkheíon Pontou* for Nos. 1, 2, 23, 24; of *Thrakiká*, for No. 3; of the *Arkheíon tou Thrakikoú laographikoú kai glossikoú Thisauroú*, for No. 20; of *Mikrasiatiká Khroniká*, for Nos.

16, 22; of *Laographía*, for Nos. 14, 15; of *Pontiaká Phylla*, for Nos. 13, 17. Further to Dr. Mikhaïlídis-Nouáros for No. 21, and to Madame Eirini Moskóvi for No. 12*b*.

The Delegates of the Clarendon Press have treated me with their usual consideration, and the Staff of the Press with their expected accuracy and attention. Nor must I forget my friend Sir William Halliday, who nearly forty years ago set my feet on the flowery paths of Greek story-telling, by careful criticism has always helped me, and to this present book has contributed a great deal more than he would like me to express in this preface.

R. M. D.

Contents

ABBREVIATIONS ix

LIST OF STORIES

1. *The little Boy and his elder Sister* 1
2. *The three Fairies of Sandy Batoum* 5
3. *The ungrateful Snake, the Fox, and the Man* 9
4. *The Cyclops* 12
5. *The Prince in a Swoon* 25
6. *The Story of Johnnie and his younger Brother* 30
7. *The Wild Man and his Daughter* 38
8. *Fair as the Sun* 46
9. *Fiorendino;* or *The Forgotten Bride* 55
10. *The Blessing Incarnate* 59
11. *The Boy carried away to the World Below* 71
12. *The Sun rises in the West;* better called *The two Bets* 77
13. *The Man who pretended to be dead* 87
14. *The loving Brothers* 89
15. *The two Kings* 93
16. *Do neither Kindness nor yet Unkindness* 103
17. *The jealous Sisters* 108
18. *The fated Marriage* 112
19. *Luck and Good Sense* 115
20. *The too lucky Man* 119
21. *St. George and the Dragon* 123

22. *The Robber Captain* 129

23. *The Herb of Love* 137

24. *The two Pauls* 155

25. *The Next World* 164

26. *The Man who would avoid Death* 172

ADDENDA TO *MODERN GREEK FOLKTALES* 174

INDEX 177

Abbreviations

Forty-five Stories = *Forty-five Stories from the Dodekanese*, by R. M. Dawkins.

Kamboúroglou = *Παραμύθια, ὑπὸ Δ. Γρ. Καμπούρογλου*, Athens, 1912.

Kanellákis. This refers to a manuscript collection of folktales from Chios recorded by Konstantinos N. Kanellákis, probably in the latter years of the nineteenth century. It is in the hands of Dr. Philip Argenti, who kindly allows me to make use of these stories.

M.G.F. = *Modern Greek Folktales*, chosen and translated by R. M. Dawkins.

M.G. in A.M. = *Modern Greek in Asia Minor*, by R. M. Dawkins.

1

The little Boy and his elder Sister

THE present story has been analysed in *M.G.F.*, No. 2, where it is shown to have two forms: in one, characteristic of western and northern Greece, the girl is called Pleiad and her brother Star of Dawn; after their troubles they are carried away to heaven by God, and the sister is made a Pleiad and her brother the morning star. Of this a variant from Zákynthos is there printed, but nothing to represent the eastern version, the story as it is found in Asia Minor and the islands: for this reason a variant from Pontos has been chosen for this book. The main difference between the two versions is in the ending. In the eastern version the children, here called Yanníkas and Maríka, Johnnie and Polly, after running away, are persecuted, either by the mother of the young man who marries the sister, or, as in the present version, by the witch who has induced the girl to come down from the tree. The details vary, but generally, as in the present variant, the girl is turned into a fish and in some way delivered by her brother, who has become a deer. His fate seems always to be left obscure, but the girl is restored to her place by her royal husband and the jealous witch duly punished.

Commonplaces of Greek and other story-telling are the magical pursuit, with the evasion by transformations, and the way in which the girl is forced to come down from the tree: she feels she must put the old woman right when she sees her doing a simple thing in exactly the wrong way.

This is a real fairy-tale told to amuse children, who would naturally be interested in the adventures of the two children so very much like themselves. Such entirely childish stories are not so very common in Greece.

NO. 1. THE LITTLE BOY AND HIS ELDER SISTER[1]

There was once an old man and an old woman, and they had two little children, Johnnie and Polly. One day they gave the children some milk bread to eat and themselves went off to

[1] Text from Santa in Pontos, printed in *Arkheion Pontou*, i. 197.

fetch water. While the parents were filling their jars, they began to think, and they said: 'How long must we old folks go on supporting these children? Maybe they will live and grow big, but then when they are big, God knows if they will look after us. Let us kill them and then when they are dead, we shall be free of it all.'

While Johnnie and Polly were eating, a crow passed that way croaking out: 'Kra, kra; I know, I know!' 'And what do you know?' said Johnnie. 'If you will give me some milk bread, then I will tell you.' Johnnie had already finished his bread, but he took a piece from Polly and gave it to the crow, saying: 'And what do you know, you crow?' 'If you go home, your parents will kill you dead; see you don't go!' Johnnie and Polly at once and in great haste went into the house, and took away with them everything which the crow had told them to take: carding combs, needles, soap, oil, spindle whorls, curds, and ashes; so they ran off.

When the old man and the old woman came home and found the children not there, they saw what had happened and started to run after them. When they came close up to them, the children threw down the combs and the needles, and in front of the old man and the old woman these turned into nails and thorns, so for a while they fell behind. Yet they did pass through the thorns and almost caught up to the children, but these threw down the spindle whorls, and all the country was filled with holes and ditches, and the old man and the old woman fell down and broke their legs. Then the children went on and scattered the ashes abroad, and the dust rose up to heaven; the old people were dazzled and their eyes failed. The children threw down the soap, and it became a slippery place; the old people fell down and half killed themselves. Then the children poured out the oil and it turned into a river. They poured out the curd and it turned into a sea: the old man and the old woman didn't know what to do.

When Johnnie and Polly saw that they had escaped from the old man and the old woman, they sat down to have a rest. From so much running their clothes were dripping wet, and they were scorched with thirst. 'Oh, Polly, I am very thirsty,' said Johnnie. 'And what can we do about it? There is no water here.' The place there was all covered with the footprints of bears, and of wolves and deer. Then said Johnnie: 'Polly, I must drink from these footprints.' They were of a bear. 'Oh no,' said Polly, 'for then you will become a bear and devour me.' 'Well, let me drink from the footprint of a deer.' 'But you will be changed into a little deer and be lost in the wood, and I be left with no little brother.' Then to make him forget his thirst, she said: 'Come, Johnnie, and let me cleanse your head.' And then said Johnnie: 'Oh yes, Polly, and I will cleanse yours.' As he was doing this, Polly was so tired that she fell asleep, and then Johnnie stooped and drank water from a deer's footprint; he was turned into a little deer and lost in the wood. When Polly woke up and did not see him, she began to cry: 'Oh, alas, Johnnie, and where are you?' The little deer came and lifted her up on his horns and carried her to the top of a tall pine-tree: five men could not have got their arms round that tree. Every day the deer used to come and bring her food, one thing and another.

In that place and quite near the pine-tree there was a lake, and to it the king's horses used to come to drink. When they saw Polly's reflection in the water, they were frightened and shied away. One day the grooms went and told the king of this: 'O my king, and may your kingdom be well! Your horses every time we take them to drink begin shying and won't drink.' The king was a man of good wit, and he told them to look at the trees near by, because it might be something in the tree that was frightening the horses. When the men looked up they saw the girl. They tried to climb up the tree but they couldn't; it had no branches; and they could not get their arms round it, it was so very big. They took axes to hew at the tree and bring it down. So they hewed and hewed, but they could not hew right through it, and they had to leave a little of the trunk for the next day. In the night the little deer came and licked at the trunk and made it even thicker than it was before. They saw that they could not manage it and so they gave it up.

Somewhere near the tree there was a witch living, whose advice the king sought when he was in a difficulty. So he sent and called for the witch, and she said to him: 'I can bring that girl down from the tree.' She took a kneading trough and a sieve and some ashes and went under the pine-tree to do some sieving. She took her seat inside the kneading trough and let the sievings fall outside it. Polly from up in the pine-tree saw her and cried out: 'Auntie, auntie, you must sit outside the trough and let the sievings fall inside, and then perhaps you will be able to make a little cake.' The witch answered: 'Lower your perch, my little dove, and sit here: I am deaf; I can't hear.' In this way the witch got the girl down to the lower branches; then she caught her by the hair and dragged her down; seized her and took her off to the king. When the king saw her he fell in love with her. In joyful wedlock he made her his wife.

One day the witch out of jealousy induced the girl to come down to the lake; she gave her a push and the girl fell in. The king searched for her up and down, but he could not find her. He asked the witch, but she told him some lying tale. Every day the little deer used to throw a loaf into the lake and then go away. One day he was seen and people understood what was being done; they emptied the lake and in it found a tame fish, and in the fish's belly there was Polly. They questioned her and found out what the witch had done. The king sent for the witch and asked her: 'Would you like to go out for a ride with horses or would you rather the sword?' The witch said: 'May the sword pierce the eyes of thine enemies: I would rather ride the horses.' The men took her and tied her to the tails of the horses; they whipped up the horses, and they dragged her to her death.

2

The three Fairies of Sandy Batoum

THIS story of the three fairies of Sandy Batoum, who give the hero one after the other three bracelets, and at the end he marries the youngest and most beautiful, I do not, rather to my surprise, find anywhere else than here at Samsoun. Nor do I know if Sandy Batoum, *τὸ Κοὺμ-πατόμι*, has any connexion with the port of Batoum on the Black Sea. The story contains several elements well known in these Greek stories. The boy with an urgent task to perform who, instead of setting to work, spends the night cracking nuts and relies for the performance of his task upon some supernatural help, is perhaps most in place in *The Underworld Adventure*, for which see *M.G.F.*, No. 26. The fairies who change from doves into beautiful girls are in many stories. The fairy of the sea, who tries to sink the ship, belongs to what is left in Greek folklore of the Alexander romance: she is in various stories either the sister, the mother, or the lady-love of Alexander, who has hurled her into the sea, where she became a dangerous mermaid, because she had got before him in drinking the Water of Immortality. She asks sailors where Alexander is. If they say that he is dead she sinks the ship.[1] The Jew who makes a dishonest claim for the bracelet is equally familiar, as is the triple development of the story, but for it as a whole I find no parallels, though one surely might turn up any time, especially, one suspects, from Asia Minor.

NO. 2. THE THREE FAIRIES OF SANDY BATOUM[2]

There was once a man and his wife; both of them people who feared God. Also they had a son, he too grew up in the great fear of God. He went off and was apprenticed to the king's butcher. That very same evening the king's daughter had been betrothed, and the king said to the butcher: 'Tomorrow

[1] There is a discussion of the Lady of the Sea in a paper on 'Alexander and the Water of Life' in *Medium Aevum*, vi, especially p. 185.

[2] Text from Samsoun in Pontos; printed in *Arkheion Pontou*, vii. 113.

in the morning I must have forty sheep, all of them still warm.' The butcher fell into deep thought about this. The boy heard the reason and said: 'Than this can there be anything easier? Just bring me a bag of nuts and I will manage the whole matter.' From the evening right through to the morning the boy sat eating nuts; he ate them all. Then at dawn he made his prayer to God, and God heard him and brought it about that the forty sheep should be ready; all of themselves, flayed and reeking. The boy told the butcher, and the butcher brought the sheep to the king, still reeking. The butcher was so much pleased that he gave the boy his daughter in marriage, although all the time she was betrothed to another butcher. This other man wanted to bring the boy to ruin, and he said to him: 'Come, let us make up a party and go and have a meal out in the country in the meadows.' In the place where they went there was opposite them a vine, and it bore grapes both winter and summer. The man, who was with the boy, said to him: 'Go and bring some of the grapes from there for us to eat.' Now whoever went to that place never came back again.

The boy came near and climbed up the vine. On the ground below him there came a fairy, and when the boy saw her, he came down and caught her by the hair and smote her to the ground. She changed from a girl into a dove; with him she left a golden bracelet, saying: 'Whoever searches for me will find me, at Sandy Batoum.' The boy took the bracelet and put it in his bosom. The man who had been with him ran off, and the boy gathered a few grapes and went off home again.

In the morning the king called for the butcher and said to him: 'You must now bring me what you owe me, three hundred and fifty gold pieces.' The butcher at this fell into deep thought, and the boy questioned him. Then said his father-in-law: 'My debt to the king is three hundred and fifty gold pieces, and I have not wherewith to pay him.' Then said the boy: 'Take this bracelet and go and sell it and so pay your debt.' The man went into the market to sell the bracelet. A Jew saw it in his hand and said to him: 'Where did you find this thing? It belongs to me.' Then the Jew went to the law-court and summoned the butcher. Then they called for the son-in-law of the butcher and asked him where he had found the bracelet: it belonged to the Jew. The boy said: 'It is mine, and grant me a delay of forty days and I will go and fetch another onc like it.'

The boy came to a shore of the sea and there he saw a ship. He waved his kerchief and a boat came out from the ship and took him on board. Full in the midst of the sea there was a fairy; all the ships sailing by she sank. They passed close by and the fairy seized the rudder to sink the ship. The boy caught her by the hair and threw her down. Then the fairy turned into a dove and flew off, leaving with him a golden bracelet, and saying: 'Whoever seeks for me will find me, at Sandy Batoum.' The boy took the bracelet and put it in his pocket.

The ship went on and set the boy ashore in a city. There he went to the house of an old woman and in the night he started singing. The old woman said to him: 'Don't do that; the son of the king here has had a stroke; it took him suddenly and he died, and even now they are burying him.' Then the boy said: 'Come now, show me the tomb.' The old woman brought him to the tomb. The boy dug a hole in it; he looked in and saw a fairy; she was sporting with the king's son. He caught her by the hair and felled her to the ground. From a girl she changed into a dove and flew off, leaving with him a bracelet. She said: 'Whoever seeks for me will find me, at Sandy Batoum.' The boy put the bracelet in his pocket. Then he brought the king's son out of the grave and carried him to his father. The king questioned him: 'Ask of me whatever gift you like.' The boy said: 'Find me a man to take me to Sandy Batoum.' An old man was found who said: 'I know the way to Sandy Batoum.'

When they were coming near, the old man said to the boy: 'Here is the house of the fairies. Take three sheep with you; there by the gate three lions are standing; give them a sheep each.' This the boy did and then went and hid himself, making a hole to look out through. Three doves came and changed into girls; then they sat down and ate. When the eldest girl was drinking wine, her two sisters asked her: 'Tell us, what did you see when you were away two months ago?' Then she said: 'While I was standing underneath a vine, a young man came and gripped me by the hair and struck me to the ground: to the health of that young man I drink this wine.' Saying this, she drank up the wine. Then the middle sister said: 'When I was staying full in the midst of the sea, a youth gripped me by the hair and struck me down; to the health of that youth I am drinking this wine.' Saying this, she drank up the wine. Then came the turn of the youngest girl, and she said: 'When I was in the tomb sporting with the king's son, a youth came and gripped me by the hair and struck me to the ground; to the health of that youth I too drink the wine.'

Then the youth showed himself and said: 'I am that boy.' Then they embraced him and kissed him; they asked him: 'Why have you come here?' The boy said: 'To get still more bracelets.' And the girls gave him them in plenty. In the morning he got up to go his way. The eldest girl said to her lion: 'In how many hours can you carry this youth to his city?' The lion said: 'In three hours.' Then the second sister asked her lion, and he said: 'In two hours.' Then the youngest asked her lion, and he said: 'I can carry him there in half an hour.' Then the youth mounted on the youngest sister's lion and in half an hour the lion carried him to his city. The lion turned back and the youth went to his palace. He summoned the Jew, and he took and set the bracelet the Jew had claimed among the other bracelets and said to him: 'Now recognize your own bracelet.' And the Jew said: 'How do I know which it is? They are all the same.' Then the Jew was hanged, and for the boy they began to hold for forty days and for forty nights a joyous wedding feast. He was among the bran and we among the flour; he had eggs by the sieveful and we money by the bagful.

3

The ungrateful Snake, the Fox, and the Man

ON this story, seemingly from the East, Politis has written in *Laographía*, ii. 160, and Halliday has a note in *M.G. in A.M.*, p. 245. The story falls into two parts: in the first the man by the cunning of the Fox is able to destroy the ungrateful Snake; in the second part, which is sometimes lacking, we have the ingratitude of the man to the Fox, when she comes to claim her promised reward. In the version from Thrace, which I print here, the animals speak in character: the matter-of-fact ass, the generous horse, and the cunning Fox, who turns everything to her own advantage, until at the end she is worsted by the still greater artfulness of the man.

The Greek variants are:

1. PONTOS: *Istoría kai statistikí tis Trapezoúntos*, by Savvas Ionídis, 1870, p. 266.
2, 3. CAPPADOCIA: *M.G. in A.M.*, pp. 335, 429.
4. INDJE SOU, near Kaisariyeh: Carnoy et Nicolaïdes, *Traditions populaires de l'Asie Mineure*, p. 238.
5. THRACE: *Thrakiká*, xvii. 108. Here translated.
6. EPEIROS: Hahn, No. 87 (ii. 95).
7. DORIS: reference in *Laographía*, ii. 161, to G. Koutra, *90 Mourapádes*, Athens, 1899, pp. 3–7. Inaccessible to me.
8. LECCE: Morosi, *Studi sui dialetti greci*, p. 75.

NO. 3. THE UNGRATEFUL SNAKE, THE FOX, AND THE MAN[1]

One day a man was on his way to the mountain and he saw on the slope a big tree set on fire, and he heard a wild hissing. He went up and saw among the branches a great snake about to be burnt. When the snake saw the man he begged him to save him, and the man was sorry for the snake and took a long stick and pushed it in among the twigs. The snake coiled himself round the stick, and so escaped out of the tree.

[1] Text from Thrace; printed in *Thrakiká*, xvii. 108.

Instead of being thankful to the man who had saved him, the snake coiled himself round the man to devour him; because, he said, it was also a man who had lit the fire. The man began to plead for mercy but the snake would not listen to him. Then the man said: 'Before you devour me, let us take the verdict of anyone whom we may meet.' So, the snake being coiled round the man, they met with an ass, and him they made their judge and told him what had happened. The ass gave his opinion, saying to the snake: 'You shall devour the man, for man is a creature without kindness. He loads me up, he beats me, and now he has left me here with nothing to eat. Till the very day I die, the burden of the saddle is upon me.' When the man heard this he said: 'One judge is not enough; let us go to a second.' The snake consented, and a little farther on they met a horse and told him what had happened. The horse was sorry for the man and said to the snake: 'The man did well by you; you must not devour him.' The snake would not consent to this and they agreed to go to a third judge, and as he said so it should be done.

Then on their way they saw a fox sunning herself on a rock. They went up to her. At first the fox was frightened, but when she saw the snake coiled round the man, she said: 'They must surely have some quarrel,' and so she stayed there waiting for them. When they came, the man made a sign to the fox: he held out his forefinger and then all the ten fingers together. Immediately Polly the fox understood that he was promising her a cock and with it ten hens; to this she gladly consented and listened to all the story and what the snake had said to him. 'To be a fair judge and to do no injustice to you, I must see what has happened. There is a tree just here; the snake must go up into it.' The snake went up the tree and the fox said to the man: 'Set fire to it.' The tree caught light, and just as the man was preparing to thrust his staff into the fire for the snake to escape, 'I say! what are you doing?' cried the fox. 'Let him burn, and you now go and fetch me what you promised.' The man was very happy to have escaped, and he went to his house and took a sack and ran round in the courtyard to catch the hens to carry them to the fox. His wife heard the noise the hens were making, and she came out into the yard, and when she was told why he wanted to catch them, she said: 'And did I rear them up for this, to be given to the fox? Put the dog into the bag and take that to the fox.' 'You are right, my wife,' said he. So he put the dog into the sack and loaded it up on his back, and went off to the place where the fox was waiting for him. From a long way off the fox saw him coming with his burden, and wagged her tail with delight to think that she would have the hens to eat. But presently she had to sweat, running up the hill to get away from the dog. She sat down on a rock, and beating her brow with her paw she said: 'And how was this your business, Dame Polly, to set yourself up as a judge? Was this man your dear grandfather?' And so she beat her brow, and I was standing there on one side and saw her myself.

4

The Cyclops

No folktale is better known than the story of the Cyclops Polyphemus and Ulysses, as it has been worked into the *Odyssey* by Homer. It has recently been exhaustively studied by Oskar Hackman in his *Die Polyphemsage in den Volksüberlieferungen*, published in 1904 at Helsingfors and very fully reviewed by A. van Gennep, in his *Religions, Mœurs, et Légendes*, Paris, 1908, pp. 155–64. The story has also been studied by Sir James Frazer in Appendix XIII to the Loeb edition of *Apollodoros*, 1921. In all Hackman's 221 variants the quibble with the name occurs in much less than half, and the actual use of 'No Man', which is such a characteristic of the Homeric story, occurs so far as I can find twice only: in No. 128[1] from Anjou an entirely irrelevant little story of a man who told a fairy that his name was *Personne*, and in No. 30, a story from Lapland, with a very Homeric turn: some Lapps got caught in a cave where a giant kept his flocks. One of them blinded the giant and escaped by hanging on underneath a goat. Challenged by the giant he gave his name as 'Alls Ingen'—*Just Nobody*. Except that it does not appear that the giant is one-eyed, this story is the most Homeric of all the (non-Greek) Cyclops stories, and it seems to stand quite by itself.

Of all Hackman's 221 versions only four come from the Greek world, and of these only one, Hackman's No. 2, No. 5 in my list below, from the island of Psará, is in any way to the point. We find in it a blind giant and his flock of sheep and the escape of the hero wrapped in the skin of a sheep he has killed. There is another story of the same relevance, not in Hackman but printed by Frazer, p. 439, as recorded by Drosínis from Athens (? Euboia). In it the hero blinds the one-eyed ogre with a spit and escapes in the usual way, under the belly of a great ram. This is No. 6 of the list below.

Of Hackman's other Greek examples, No. 1 from Athens and

[1] It is quoted by Hackman from P. A. Lindholm, *Hos Lappbönder*, p. 110, and is apparently the same as the Lapp story quoted by Frazer, *Apollodoros*, II. i. 423, who has it from J. C. Poestion, *Lappländische Märchen*, Vienna, 1886, p. 122.

No. 3 from Zákynthos are no more than stories of giants, and No. 125 from Mytilene is merely an anecdote of a thief who, to avoid giving his real name, said that he was *Myself*, Apatós.[1] Indeed Hackman casts his net so wide that much of his material is entirely irrelevant to the Homeric story of the Cyclops: the occurrence of any single motive is enough to put a story into his list and the actual thread of the story he is too apt not to consider at all.

Whatever may be the value of these four variants from Hackman's list, they do not exhaust the material we now have from Greece. Since he wrote, the first Greek variant to my knowledge is the story from Phárasa, No. 4 in the list below, printed in 1916. Phárasa is, or rather was, a remote Greek-speaking village in the Taurus, where I recorded the story in 1911. In it we hear of seven priests who were carried off to his house by a Cyclops. One of them he roasted and ate: the others blinded him with a spit, and escaped by getting into the skins of six sheep which they had killed, carrying off with them the rest of the flock. On the evidence which he then had before him I think that Sir William Halliday in his comments on this story in *M.G. in A.M.*, p. 217, was fully justified in saying that it was very unlikely that this story was a survival from the ancient world. But when the stories I had collected in Asia Minor were put into Halliday's hands I was unaware that two versions of the Polyphemus story, one from Kerasund and one from Trebizond, had long before been printed, and they, I think, put the matter in quite a different light. They appeared in what is now an extremely rare periodical, the *Astír tou Pontou*, The Star of Pontos, of which only two volumes ever appeared; printed at Trebizond in 1884 and 1886. I find them now transcribed in my old notebooks of nearly fifty years ago from the copy in the National Library at Athens: they are Nos. 1 and 2 in the list below, and I print as 4 *a* the Kerasund text.

Which of the two versions I chose would have made no difference whatever, for they are almost verbally identical. A few minutiae of dialect assure us of their local character and there are a few differences in vocabulary, but the sentences are precisely alike and in only one place is there a sentence in the one that has not its counterpart in the other. From this one important

[1] The references are: No. 1 from Athens is No. 1 in Kamboúroglou; No. 3 from Zákynthos is from Bernard Schmidt, *Griechische Märchen*, No. 13, and its irrelevance is admitted even by Hackman; No. 125 from Mytilene was printed in translation by W. H. D. Rouse, in *Folklore*, vii. 154.

conclusion may be drawn. Both the narrators knew the story almost word for word, and that this should be so in two places as wide apart as Kerasund and Trebizond suggests that it must have been in verbal circulation for a very long time; long enough to have evolved a sort of fixed and final version. We see at once how very much more Homeric these Pontic versions are than any of the other Greek versions we have been considering. The No Man episode is here and in Homer, and nowhere else except in the story from Lapland and the quite irrelevant story from Anjou; the men are not priests as in the Phárasa story but shipwrecked sailors; the method of escape is also on Homeric lines. The version is, I think, a genuine survival.

At this point we may consider what was the original home of the Cyclops. From the resemblance between the Homeric story and certain versions from the Caucasus Hackman thinks that the original home of the story is in Asia Minor, and Van Gennep in his review of Hackman's book takes this same view. It may be traced even farther east. Hackman's No. 8 is a story taken from a Mongolian book of perhaps the fourteenth century in which we hear of a hero Bissat, who killed a monster who had a single eye in the crown of his head and is therefore called a Depe Ghoz, and escaped in the skin of one of his flock of sheep. This monster was called a Depe Ghoz, Eye in his Crown, because he had one eye only, and that set in the crown of his head. The people from whom this story comes are the Oghuz, a Turkish-speaking people of western Turkestan. This story with full references is given by Frazer on p. 452 of his *Apollodoros*. This and the Caucasus and Asia Minor variants make it seem that the Cyclops story drifted from the east into the Homeric world.

A word may be added about the word used for Cyclops; Tepekózis or Tepekó-is; in the Oghuz story Depe Ghoz. This is of course Turkish: from *göz* an eye and *tepe*, the word for a hillock, used also to mean the crown of the head. It therefore means a man with an eye on the crown of his head, and not, as we commonly think of the Cyclops, with an eye in the centre of his forehead. This explains the passage in the text of 4 *a*, where we are told that 'he held his head bowed downwards and this was the way in which he saw'. If he had not held his head bowed he would of course with his eye in his crown have seen nothing but the sky.

If these two stories, Nos. 1 and 2, or rather these two recordings of one and the same Cyclops story, are to be regarded as survivals from ancient Greece, we can hardly deny the same position to a story recorded certainly more than fifty years ago by I. G. Valavánis from the district of Kerasund, although it is distinctly less Homeric than the stories I have just been considering. It is No. 3 on the list and a translation is printed below as 4 *b*. We have no longer the two shipwrecked sailors, but the heroes are a poor tinsmith and another poor man: rather unusually we are told their names; the tinsmith was Yeríkas, which is for George, and his companion Leftéris, which is more obviously Elefthérios. They were so poor that they went out together to find at least something to eat. They fell in with a one-eyed man-eating ogre, a *drakos*, and he took them off to his house. When they were asleep the ogre cut Leftéris's throat, and Yeríkas, playing the part of Ulysses, blinded the ogre with a hot spit. Then he found himself in the dairy shut up among the sheep. The ogre expected to find him as the sheep went out to graze by finding among their hoofs the feet of a man. But he found no feet, for the artful Yeríkas was riding on the back of the ram with his feet well off the ground. With all the ogre's sheep following him, Yeríkas returned to the village, and collected a huge army of villagers who went and killed the ogres, fifteen households of them. Except that there is no No Man episode and the two men are not sailors the whole story is quite along the lines of Homer. Further, these three stories from Pontos, Nos. 1, 2, and 3, cast a fresh light on the Phárasa story, No. 4, and we see that it is not merely a random story about a one-eyed giant, but a poor relation of these much more Homeric versions from Pontos. From the dialect it seems very likely too that the Phárasa people at some time formed a part of Pontic Hellenism.

Most giants in story are solitary creatures, but in the story just quoted we hear of fifteen households of the one-eyed giants, and in the Pontic story, No. 46 in *M.G.F.*, *The Girl who went to war*, the Tepekóz were a whole army. So too of the Cyclops in Homer; he was of the people of the Cyclopes. This not being one man but one of a tribe or nation is a marked link between the ancient Cyclopes and their modern representatives.

A good many Polyphemus stories have a further episode. When the Cyclops has been blinded and wants to lay hands on the man, he offers him a ring which the man, drawn by its beauty, accepts. But the ring is enchanted and as soon as it is on the man's finger it begins to shout: 'Here I am! Here I am!' and by this the Cyclops hopes to locate the man who had blinded him. To free himself from this danger, the man gets rid of the ring by cutting off his finger. This episode I observe is common in European versions and oddly enough it is in the Oghuz story, but it does not occur in any of these Greek stories any more than in Homer. The No Man episode is one point they have in common; this is another.

For convenience I print here a list of these Greek versions:

1. PONTOS. Kerasund. Recorded by I. G. Valavánis and printed in the *Astír tou Pontou*, i (1884), p. 135. Translated below as 4 *a*.
2. PONTOS. Trebizond. Recorded by I. Parkharídis, and printed in *Astír tou Pontou*, i. 72. Almost identical with No. 1.
3. PONTOS. Kerasund. Recorded by I. G. Valavánis; in manuscript at Athens. Translated here as 4 *b*.
4. CAPPADOCIA. Phárasa. Printed with translation in *M.G. in A.M.*, p. 551, and reprinted by Frazer, p. 438.
5. PSARÁ. Translated in L. Ross's *Erinnerungen*, p. 281. This is No. 2 in Hackman's list, the only one in it I find relevant.
6. EUBOIA. Put into German by Drosínis in his *Land und Leute in Nord-Euboia*, p. 179. This is inaccessible to me.

These Cyclops stories seem to show the possibility of the survival of ancient Greek stories into the modern world, and the best way to throw further light on the question seems to be to bring together other possible cases.

In Aitolia and also in Macedonia we have what may well be a survival of the story of Meleager and his death, when the sympathetic brand with which his life was bound up was thrown into the fire by his mother.[1] The three Fates, we read, were present at the birth of a baby, and the decree of the third Fate was that the child should live as long as a brand then lying half burnt on the hearth should not be fully consumed. The mother preserved the brand carefully; so far we have a close parallel with the story of Meleager and Althaia. At this point, however, the ancient and the modern stories diverge. In some of the modern stories the man quarrelled with his wife, and she, knowing his secret, threw the brand into the fire. In others the man was released from a long and painful death agony by his friends in mercy burning the brand. The real claim for this story being a survival is its rarity and its local connexion with Aitolia; further that there seems to be no other Greek example of the location of the external soul of the hero in a half-burnt brand. Yet on the most favourable view we have here a survival, not of a complete story, but only of this one episode in the story of Meleager.

[1] For the Meleager story see *Folklore*, lix. 56, and *Laographía*, xi. 270.

In 1914 I recorded in Pontos two stories which are here relevant.[1] In one of them, from the village of Santa near Trebizond, we hear of a daughter who saved her lover from the pursuit of her father by throwing her brother on a fire; while the father was saving his son, the two lovers made their escape, much as Jason and Medea escaped while their pursuers were gathering up from the sea the scattered limbs of her brother Absyrtos. The other story is from the village of Imera near Argyropolis. It contains an episode of rejuvenation and by the agency of the devil a subsequent failure, which may remind us of how Medea with her magic cauldron beguiled the daughters of Aietes to kill their father by promising that she would bring him back not only to life but to youthful vigour, as she had the old ram upon which they had experimented. The unusual motives, the scattering of the body and the rejuvenation, and the localizing of the stories to the very land of Medea, form their strongest claim to be survivals; but again, as in the Meleager story, there is no question of the survival of a complete story but only of single episodes.

A much stronger case can be made out for the survival in Kos of the story of Erysichthon.[2] In a collection of stories recorded some fifty years ago in the Dodekanese we find a story from Kos called after the two kingdoms concerned, Myrmidoniá and Pharaoniá: in publishing it, text and translation, I suggested that a better title would be *The Fairy's Revenge*. The main thread of the story is that a presumptuous prince cut down the grove of trees in which a fairy had her habitation. She avenged the injury by afflicting him with the disease of ravening hunger, of which he died miserably. All his money he had spent in satisfying his appetite: 'In a few years he had consumed all his possessions and was left in poverty, always hungry. . . . Then he began to tear at his own flesh and eat it, insomuch that he died, his nails actually in his mouth.' This is quite recognizably the story of Erysichthon as found in the *Metamorphoses* of Ovid and as the main subject of Callimachus' *Hymn to Demeter*.[3] The case is the stronger because the story, apparently originating in Thessaly, seems to have become localized at the Cnidian promontory, that is at a point very close to the islands of the Dodekanese. It may also be noted that though the modern story has more of Ovid than of Callimachus,

[1] *Folklore*, lix. 57.

[2] *Forty-five Stories*, No. 33, pp. 334–49, where the details of the story are discussed.

[3] For which see especially Wilamowitz-Moellendorf, *Hellenistische Dichtung*, pp. 34–44.

it contains points, some from one and some from the other of these two authors. The conclusion seems inescapable that the story has not been taken from some learned man who had been reading Callimachus but is a local survival of the ancient legend.

In the same collection there is another story from Kos which has some claim to be regarded as a survival. The wise physician Askloup, the name being a Turkish adaptation of Asklepios, saved a king from a many-headed snake; then he wanted to marry the king's daughter, who, though so much younger, had reminded him of a girl he once loved, but had then been changed into a bird so that he lost her.[1] There was a medieval story of a daughter, not, it is true, of Asklepios but of Hippokrates, who was a snake or dragon: Mandeville calls her the Lady of Lango, by which he means Kos. In this confused tangle I cannot trace anything except the name Asklepios that is definitely ancient, and yet it is difficult not to think that the modern story must have some connexion with the healing god Asklepios, whose famous sanctuary in Kos has recently been excavated.

To what I wrote on this problem in *Forty-five Stories* I can only add a venturesome conjecture. In Giustiniani's *Istoria di Scio*, written in 1596, we find a long story about a king of Chios called Schlirionte, whose daughter was wooed by a certain Dragon King, *Re Dragone*.[2] Giustiniani can hardly be called an accurate writer, and I have a suspicion that Schlirionte, for all that it is glossed by *cioè crudele*, as if it were from σκληρός, may yet be a corruption of Asklepios, a P having been read as if it were a capital rho.

Further than this I can hardly go. Lenormant's idea that Demeter survives in a story he heard at Eleusis about a woman called Demetra leaves me incredulous.[3] Herodotus' Thief in the King's Treasury is a dip into the general store of Greek and non-Greek stories, both of the ancient and now of the modern world, and the same may be said of the story of Cupid and Psyche. Of the story of Apollonios of Tyre we have several versions in modern Greek, but it seems that they none of them derive from the ancient Greek and then Latin novel, all of them being from a rhymed Greek version taken from the Latin and printed at Venice for the first time in 1534.[4] There are not a few folktale motives

[1] *Forty-five Stories*, Nos. 34 and 34 *a*, pp. 350–6, where the necessary references are collected.

[2] In Argenti's edition, Cambridge, 1943, the story of King Schlirionte is pp. 92 and 122 ff.

[3] *Folklore*, lix. 55.

[4] This is treated in *Forty-five Stories*, No. 45, *The Story of Jack*.

common to the stories of ancient and of modern Greece and, we have a conspectus of them in Ch. X of Professor H. J. Rose's *A Handbook of Greek Mythology*, but of definite stories with similar plots I can find no more than those I have just described. Each case must be judged on its own merits.

NO. 4 *a*. THE CYCLOPS: THE GIANT WITH AN EYE IN THE CROWN OF HIS HEAD[1]

Once upon a time when a ship was somewhere on her way there arose by night a great storm, and the ship was sunk. All who were in her were drowned; two men only succeeded in laying hold of a big plank; on this they sat and the waves carried them along. It was night, and they could not see where the sea was taking them. Presently the weather became fair and the sea calm, and a long way off the men saw some mountains: this filled them with joy. Paddling with their hands like oars, after some time they made a landing.

Then said they, being faint with hunger: 'Come, let us go and see if perhaps we can find something to eat.' They went off this way and that, but they could see neither men nor houses. At last they found a cave. 'Let us go inside,' they said: 'Perhaps we shall find something there.' Then they went into the cave, and what did they see? A great big bowl full of porridge and another still bigger bowl full of milk. Eagerly they rushed up to the bowls to eat something, but presently they said: 'And what if we eat and the man who owns the cave comes and is angry with us? what if he is an ogre and devours us in his fury? Come, let us wait a little and then perhaps he will come, whoever he may be.' So they waited and waited and no one came, and they were so mad to eat that their eyes started from their heads. 'Come,' said they, 'Let us eat just a little, and then we can again wait for a while, and if anyone comes, we can ask his pardon and he will not do anything to us.' So said they. 'And then if there is any rain to fall, why, let it fall. Is not this better than to die of hunger?' So presently they ate a little porridge and drank a little milk and satisfied their hunger. How much did

[1] Pontic text from Kerasund; printed in *Astir tou Pontou*, i (1884), p. 135.

they eat? The bowls were enormous. Then they sat there and waited for the man who was the master of the cave.

In the evening they saw a long way off a man coming; he was very tall and was driving before him a flock of sheep: he was coming down towards them from the mountains. He had one eye; it was on the top of his head and as big as that! He held his head bowed downwards and this was the way in which he saw. He was a Cyclops. Presently he came quite close to the cave and the men were trembling with fear; what the poor unlucky fellows could do they did not know. Then the man came to put his sheep into the cave. When he saw the men he was very well pleased. 'Now, how did it come about that you chanced to come here?' he asked them. Then they told him all that had happened. 'We were dead of hunger and we ate a little porridge and drank a little milk, and please do not be angry with us.' The man just wanted an excuse to be angry with them, and so he said: 'Why were you eating my food? And for that I will now eat you.' He dragged them into the cave with his sheep, and closed the entrance with a huge stone so that they could not get it open. Then he asked them: 'What is your name?' One of them told his name, and the other who had more of the devil in him said: 'No Man is what they call me.'

Then the Cyclops swallowed all the bowl of porridge and gulped down all the milk at one breath. Then he kindled the fire and laid a spit across it. When all was hot, he put a sheep on the spit and roasted it over the fire and stuffed it all into his mouth and swallowed it. Then again he got the spit hot and went and spitted on it the body of the man who had told his name. He cooked him over the fire a little and him too he ate right up. Then again he set the spit over the fire to get hot so he could devour the other man. Then he said: 'Now we will lie down for a little rest and then get up and devour him.' The other poor fellow was trembling with fear, saying to himself: 'Soon this man will devour me too; and what am I to do?' Then the Cyclops stretched himself out to take a little rest: he shut his eye and began to snore. When the man saw him lying down and sound asleep, he went and took the spit from the fire, and when it was very hot, he came quietly up to him and thrust it right through his eye and blinded him. The monster jumped up and ran this way and that, shouting with pain and trying to catch the man. But this way and that the man ran off into the corners of the cave in behind the sheep and was not to be caught. After a while the Cyclops saw that he could not catch him, and he went outside the cave, trampling about and searching for him. Then presently—and oh what a sight for your eyes!—there came together some five or ten one-eyed giants and when they saw that he had been blinded they asked: 'Who is it that has blinded you?' The Cyclops said: 'No Man has blinded me.' The others said to one another: 'If it be that no man has blinded him, then it must be God who has blinded him; come, let us go our way.' And so they went off. The Cyclops would say nothing more to them; he was afraid too that they might find the man and devour him themselves. Then he went back into his cave and searched and sought for the man and again he could not catch him.

Then the dawn came and the sheep began to be uneasy, bleating *Ba Ba*, and the Cyclops became aware that it was day. He said: 'Now when I am leading out the sheep I will stand over them at the entrance and if the man comes to try to pass out, I will catch him; and if he is not there, I will again block up the entrance and go into the cave and there it will be quite easy to catch him.' Then he opened the entrance to the cave and stood by it, and every single sheep as it passed out he felt with his hands. With the sheep the man went to the entrance, and when he saw a big ram on his way through, he got underneath him and there on his hands and knees went out himself, and the Cyclops was not aware of him. When the man had passed through the entrance he went off to the shore at a run. When the Cyclops had let all the sheep out of the cave, he searched for the man; all in vain, he could not find him. When the man had got down to the shore, he saw a ship and signed to her with his hand; the sailors came on shore and took him on board and he went off on his way.

NO. 4 *b*. THE MAN WHO BLINDED THE OGRE: A CYCLOPS STORY[1]

There was once a tinsmith; a poor man and he had nothing to eat. He met another poor man and to him he said: 'Up! Let us be going to some foreign land and make some money. Will you come?' 'I will,' said the man. So they went and went, five days on the road, and their provisions came to an end and they were very hungry. They were still going on, when they met an ogre and cried out to him: 'Tonight will you give us a lodging?' The ogre shouted to them furiously: 'I *will* give you a lodging,' and with his hands he made a sign to them. They went up to him, and when they came a little close and saw him clearly, they said to one another: 'Alas for us! This is one of those ogres and he will devour us. God have mercy upon us!' One of them—this was Leftéris—said: 'Let us run away.' 'How can we run away?' said the tinsmith: this was Yeríkas. 'Three feet and he will catch us. Let us go up to him and God will give us some way to escape. If we try to run away we shall do very ill. Even if he devours us, he will first give us something to eat, and we are dead of hunger.' So they went up to the ogre, and he took them off to his house and brought them something to eat that had been cooked with man's blood. Then not to eat they were afraid, and were they to eat, the food was not eatable. The younger man, Leftéris, ate but with loathing; the elder man, Yeríkas, put the food into his mouth and, without the ogre seeing him, took it out and threw it down under the table. When they had finished the ogre took them into his house. He lit the fire and laid down bedding both for them and for himself. While the men were thinking what they should do, the ogre rose and brought down from the shelf the hand of a man; he set it on the coals to cook it, and then he would eat it. As soon as the men saw the hand they fell to weeping. The ogre cooked it and ate it just close to them. Then he lay down on his bed and slept, though this was only a pretence.

The men stretched themselves out on their beds, and Yeríkas said to Leftéris: 'Let one of us sleep and the other

[1] Text from Kerasund; in manuscript at Athens.

keep watch; in turns, an hour each.' They could not run away, for the ogre had set up against the door a stone of maybe three thousand okes. Yeríkas went to sleep for an hour; in his turn he woke up Leftéris. At a time when Yeríkas was watching, the ogre rose up very quietly and sharpened his knife and then came to kill them. He pushed Yeríkas's legs and perceived that he was awake. Then he pushed Leftéris's legs and saw that he was asleep. He was afraid to kill them while they were awake in case the other ogres should hear and come and devour the men themselves. Very quietly he lifted aside the bedclothes and cut Leftéris's throat. Then Yeríkas jumped up and went and sat by the fire. There was a big spit there and Yeríkas privily laid it on the fire. While the spit was heating, the ogre had started nodding and had shut his eye. Those ogres had one eye only and in their forehead. Yeríkas went up to him very quietly, and squish! drove the spit into the ogre's eye. The ogre was blinded and cried out wildly and jumped up to kill Yeríkas. But first here and then there, the man ran away and the ogre could not catch him. Yeríkas went into a hole to hide and the ogre thought he had gone out of the house. He took the stone from the door and, as he was looking outside, Yeríkas came out and went into the sheepfold among the ogre's sheep. The ogre looked for him in vain. Then he set the stone up against the door of the sheepfold, and Yeríkas was left shut up inside among the sheep.

When it was dawn the ogre took away the stone that he might take count of the sheep as they went out, and if his hands fell upon a man's foot, then he would devour him. Yeríkas caught hold of the fleece of the big ram and rode mounted on his back, and so he went out of the door and started to go away on the road by which he had come. Then all the sheep followed after the big ram: the sheep were about five hundred. While Yeríkas was going off, the other ogres thought that their companion had taken his sheep and was going off to graze them. The ogres shouted to Yeríkas: 'Come and let us have a dance and make merry.' The ogres made merry and so did he, but he was saying: 'O God, I hope they won't come near me.'

So Yeríkas went on and on and came to his village. And when they saw the sheep the people said: 'When did this man get all these sheep? It is not yet twenty days since he went away.' Then they asked him: 'What did you do to get them all and so quickly?' He said: 'I have now no time to tell you this. First bring me something to eat.' When he had eaten he said: 'Now I shall lie down to sleep and do not wake me up, and when I get up I will tell you.' He lay down and went to sleep for three days and three nights. Then he got up and his neighbours came to see him, and he told them all the things we have been telling you. They went and told the king and he sent to proclaim that everyone from fifteen to seventy years old should assemble. They were a company of about fifteen thousand men, and the king said to them: 'You must go off with Yeríkas there, and go and kill all the ogres.' These ogres were about fifteen households. The company of men went and said to Yeríkas: 'Come; and let us go together to kill the ogres. We don't know the way.' Yeríkas said: 'I can't come; I am afraid of the ogres.' 'Don't be afraid,' said they, and set him right in the middle of the company, and so they went off. He showed them the house of the ogre who had devoured Leftéris. The men, while the ogres were asleep, locked up all the doors of their houses and shot at the ogres with arrows: in those days there were no guns. The people turned back but Yeríkas, as soon as he reached his house, died. The sheep were left for his wife and his children.

5

The Prince in a Swoon

MOST that needs to be said about this story, of which a version from Skopelos is now printed, I have said in the introduction to the version from Skyros in *M.G.F.*, No. 32. In Greece I find seven versions scattered from the islands to Epeiros. It has not, as yet, been recorded from Asia Minor, although an Indian origin has been suspected by Cosquin, and Lorimer has a version from Persia,[1] and of course fresh versions may turn up at any time. The story is generally well told. When the bird tells the heroine, 'a man who 's dead shall be your lot,' the prophecy must be taken to mean a man who has already in a manner passed from life to death in a magic swoon.

In the episode of the girl consulting the three symbolic gifts I have corrected the text which mentions the Rope twice and leaves out the Knife. I cannot avoid the feeling that in the story as originally designed each of the three gifts successively gives an answer to the girl's question of what she should do and each of these corresponds to her successive reactions towards her unfaithful husband. The first is anger, and the Knife gives the answer that she should kill him. The second reaction, after the first burst of anger, is that the girl feels despair, and to this the Rope can only answer that she should hang herself. Then the violence of her feelings is relaxed, and the Stone reminds her that patience is the answer to all troubles. Just as this is dawning on her, she sees her husband by her side, and he has at last understood what has happened. This same incident of the Knife and the Rope and the Stone of Patience have been worked into a version of *Snow-white* recorded in Chios, and printed by Argenti and Rose, i. 498.

From the sentence in the story: 'if anyone separates a man from his wife, &c.', one can see how terrible this is in Greek ideas. In *M.G.F.*, No. 82, I have printed a story called 'The greater Sinner', and in it we see that the wickedest thing possible is to 'interfere with the goodness of God by hindering the natural blessings of abundant water and of happy marriage'.

The girl's name in Greek is Maroudítsa, a diminutive of Maria: I have ventured to translate it by Polly.

[1] Cosquin, *Contes indiens*, p. 95; Lorimer, *Persian Tales*, p. 19.

NO. 5. THE PRINCE IN A SWOON[1]

Once upon a time there was a woman and she had a daughter, called Polly. When Polly was big she went to school. One day on her way there she saw a bird, and the bird called to her: 'Polly, Polly; sew your seam or sew it not, a man who 's dead shall be your lot.' Polly heard this, but she paid no great heed to it. Again she was going by the same place—she was on her way home—and again she saw the bird. When the bird saw her, again it began: 'Polly, Polly; sew your seam or sew it not, a man who 's dead shall be your lot.' Hearing this a second time, Polly began to think about it. She went home and sat down at the table; all the time she was thinking over this matter. When her mother saw this, she asked her to tell her what she had on her mind, but she would only say: 'There is nothing the matter with me.' At last when her mother pressed her, she told her all about it. 'When I was on my way to school, I saw a bird and it cried to me: Polly, Polly; sew your seam or sew it not, a man who's dead shall be your lot.' 'Never mind, my child; it's nothing. Let the bird talk; don't you listen,' said her mother. After that they ate their meal and went to sleep.

Next morning when she got up Polly dressed herself to go to school; she took her books and went off. On the way in the same place—I have told you her path led that way—she again saw the bird, and again it cried to her: 'Polly, Polly; sew your seam or sew it not, a man who's dead shall be your lot.' Then the bird went away. Polly again began to be much troubled. She went to the school, but she didn't attend to her lessons at all. Not to make a long story of it, many days passed in this way; when Polly went to school, the bird always said to her this same thing.

One Sunday some neighbours said to Polly's mother: 'Won't you let Polly come with us to pick a few herbs and walk a little in the sunshine.' It was a very fine day of winter. Out of doors the weather was God's delight. 'Of course I can let you have her,' said her mother, and let Polly go with

[1] Text from Skopelos; printed in Kretschmer's *Der heutige lesbische Dialekt*, p. 543, No. 30.

them. As they were walking gathering herbs, they saw a long way off a great palace. 'Oh, a palace!' said one of them; 'Let 's go there!' said another girl. 'Shall we go?' 'Let us!' So said they all and set off. When they got there one girl pushed at the door to open it; another one pushed; but in vain: the door wouldn't open. Then Polly gave a push. The door opened and then shut again; Polly was shut inside. Then the girls tried to open it again, but to no purpose; the door wouldn't open.

Polly inside the palace walked on. She opened one door and found no one. She opened the next door: she found three men, all lying dead. She opened the next door and found three more. She opened the last door; there she found a man stretched out flat on a bed, and in his hand he had a paper written: 'Whoever laments for me forty days and forty nights: if it be a girl, I will take her as my wife; if it be an old woman, I will take her for my mother; if it be a youth, I shall make him my brother; and if it be an old man, I will take him as my father.' The man was a youth of about thirty years; he was the son of a king. As soon as Polly saw these things, she took thought and said: 'Now as it is, I can't get away from here; well, let me stay here and lament for him.' And she fell to lamenting.

Thirty-nine days and thirty-nine nights she lamented over the youth, never shutting an eye. Then late in the evening she rose up from his side and went out on the terrace to get a breath of air. As she was sitting there, a gipsy woman passed below her, crying out 'Scissors and pins!' When she saw Polly she said: 'My daughter, won't you let me come up to you?' Polly said: 'How can I have you up here? I can't; I don't know how.' Then the gipsy brought out a rope and said: 'Catch hold of this rope and draw me up.' So she came up. When she was up, the gipsy asked her: 'How did you come here?' Then Polly sat down and told her the whole story. When the gipsy had heard it, she said to Polly: 'My child, you must be tired. Come, you go and sleep and I will carry on the lamentation over him. When he wakes up, I will call for you and you shall take him for your husband and I will be a mother to both of you.' Polly said: 'Very well,' and then she lay down and went to sleep.

When the forty days and forty nights had come to an end, the prince rose up, and what did he see? He saw by his side a black woman with huge teeth, as hideous as you can imagine; she it was who was lamenting for him. When he saw her, he said: 'Is it you who were lamenting for me? it is you I shall take for my wife. This woman was my fate.' There, however, he saw also Polly, fallen asleep. Then he asked the gipsy: 'What is she doing here?' Said the gipsy: 'This woman I met on the road outside and was sorry for her and brought her here.' And he believed her. When the prince woke up, all the people there in the palace woke up too and came to life. All the mules began to stir and the horses and the geese and the fowls; all the men too began their business again. Then the prince asked the gipsy: 'Now for Polly here, what shall we do with her?' 'Let us set her to look after the geese,' said the gipsy, 'and to lead them out to grass.' So they set her to keep the geese. Polly took out the geese, and in a few days they were growing fat, because as Polly wept her tears were turned into pearls and the geese ate them and grew fat.

One day the prince thought to go on a journey, and he asked all his servants, both men and women: what did they want him to bring them from his travels? One said: 'I want a hat'; another an umbrella; one man wanted a coat, and another something else. He said to Polly: 'You, Polly, what do you want me to bring you?' Then the gipsy woman jumped up and said: 'There is nothing at all that Polly wants.' 'I don't want anything,' said Polly. 'What do you mean? You don't want anything?' said the prince. 'Come, tell me what is it you would like me to bring you.' 'Bring me,' said Polly, 'a Stone of Patience, a Knife of Slaughter, and a Rope of Hanging. And if it should be that you do not bring me these things, then may the sea beneath you be turned to stone.' 'Very well,' said the prince, and he went off.

So when he had finished his business and had bought all the gifts for the rest of them, the prince embarked on his ship to go back home again. But the sea had turned to stone and his ship could make no way; she stuck there where she was. Then the captain asked one of the men: 'Have you left anything undone?' Then he questioned another; 'Nothing,' said the man. Nobody had failed in any matter. Then he questioned the prince: 'Your Highness, have you left anything undone?' The prince looked in his notebook and saw that he had failed to bring what Polly had asked for. So he disembarked and went to a shop and bought the things. When he was buying them, the merchant said to him: 'You must mind and see what she will do with these things.' So the prince went back to the ship, and the sea beneath them was stone no longer, and they went off.

When the prince came to the palace, he ran quickly, one two, and gave Polly the things I have told you, and then he watched her closely to see what she would do with them, and had she anything to say. He saw her tying the rope to a tree as just about to hang herself. Then the Stone cried out to her: 'Patience, Patience!' 'But how can I be patient?' said Polly. 'I for thirty-nine days and for thirty-nine nights lamented over the body of the prince, and after that a gipsy woman came and lamented over him for one day, and now she has him for her husband and I am sent to keep the geese. Such a thing can I endure?' Then she moved towards the Knife to kill herself, and the Stone again cried out to her: 'Patience, Patience!' and she again said the same words. Then the prince ran up and caught hold of her. 'So it was you,' he said, 'who lamented over me: it is you I will have for my wife.'

Then he went up to his house and asked the gipsy woman a question: 'If anyone separates a man and his wife, tell me what is to be done to that person.' 'You are the king,' said the gipsy woman, 'and you must know what should be done to him. On each and every door in the town nail up a piece of that man; a piece no larger than an empty nutshell.' 'And that is what I shall do to you,' said he, and the little pieces he scattered all abroad. Then he married Polly and they lived well and may we live even better.

NOTE. *The text omits the Knife and mentions the Rope twice: I have made the necessary slight adjustment.*

6

The Story of Johnnie and his younger Brother

THIS story from Thera, of which I know no close variant, is on the same lines as the specifically Pontic story, of which a version from Kerasund is printed in *M.G.F.*, No. 38. Both belong to the wide group examined by Bolte and Polivka in *Anmerkungen*, i. 528, in their remarks on Grimm, No. 60, *The two Brothers*. Both the present story and the one in *M.G.F.* are based on the same theme: a clever younger brother who helps his elder through all his troubles. In both the elder marries and gets into difficulties, from which he is rescued by his junior, who in both at the end of the story finds a wife in the house of his brother's opponent. In both, the brothers are so much alike as to be taken one for the other, though in the present story the resemblance is not pressed to the point of the junior sleeping in the bed of his brother's wife with a sword laid between them. In both it is from a sympathetic token that the younger discovers his brother's peril. The principal difference is that in the present story the elder brother is in peril from the plots of his wicked mother: a point I do not find elsewhere.

The fundamental resemblance between our story and the stories of two brothers studied in *M.G.F.* are so great, while the ways in which the theme is worked out have so many differences, that it is difficult to say anything of their real relationship. To call them variants would be to go too far; to deny their fundamental resemblance is equally not possible.

The name *Athánatos* is of course Greek for Immortal. That the dead ogre should rise up again from his ashes when they are kept watered is almost a commonplace of Greek story-telling. That the food kneaded from the ogre's ashes should be fatal to everyone but his own son echoes the often found feeling of the intensely close physical contact between a father and his son, for which see No. 24 below. The choosing of a rusty weapon in preference to one of a more promising appearance is also a commonplace.

NO. 6. THE STORY OF JOHNNIE AND HIS YOUNGER BROTHER[1]

Red thread twisted well,
Neatly wound upon the reel;
Kick the reel to make it spin,
Then the tale may well begin.

There was once a king who had three sons, and the youngest son his parents loved well. When he grew big he said to his mother: 'Mother, come, let us go away together, will you?' Before this his father had died and his brothers too and he and his mother were left alone: he took her and they went off together. Their way led through the wood, and they walked on all day and all night, and they were still among the trees when the dawn came. In that place the young prince saw a palace. He left his mother among the trees and went forward. There he saw an ogre, and this was the king of the ogres. He said: 'What do you want here, boy?' The boy said: 'I have come here to wrestle with you.' 'But I am a great ogre and you are a little boy; how can you match yourself with me? But if you can, come into the hall of the palace and we will wrestle.' So they wrestled and the boy knocked a dint in the ground and forced the ogre deep down into it.

Then he went off and left his mother in the palace, saying to her: 'Mother, you stay here and I will go and shoot birds for us to eat. But look here, mother. Never let water fall on this place here, because inside down below there is an ogre and he will come to life and come out.' She said: 'Very well, my boy.' So off he went with his weapons and brought back birds, and they cooked and ate them. But when her son said this to her and had one day gone off, the woman said: 'But I must look into the matter and pour out a little water over the place and see what this can be.' She filled a pitcher and poured the water out over the place. Then her son came and they ate the birds he brought. Every day she used to pour water over the place, and the ogre refreshed by the water came out. When he appeared he said: 'O my darling, it was

[1] Text from Thera; printed in *Doffner's Archiv*, i. 133.

you who with this water gave me life; that life we must live together.' She said: 'Yes, indeed; I had need of company, and now you are here.' Her son saw this, and whenever the ogre came he used quietly to lie hidden in a room. One day passed and another and the queen became with child by the ogre. Her son saw this and would say to her: 'O my mother, how stout you are getting with the birds I bring you every day.' All the same he knew what was going on, but he did not want to let her see this. Her month came, and one day her son said to her: 'My mother, you are about to have a child, and if you give me a sister, I will kill her and you too; if you give me a brother, I will do all I can for you and love you well. Also, my mother, I have found someone to help you at the birth. Yet if the baby be a sister, you must go away right out of my sight: you are as good as dead.' Two or three days after this the pains came upon her. When her son was aware of this, he went away into the forest, that he might neither hear nor see anything. His mother had a male child. When the child was born it was laid underneath the table; they took it and set it on the table. The son heard of all this and went into the house and saw the child on the table. He went and put his arms round him and kissed him. 'Now, mother, I shall love you even more.' Johnnie himself asked leave to hold the boy at the font. 'What name?' Then he said: 'Athánatos: he who knows not death.' Food was brought for the child, and Athánatos made a good meal. Johnnie loved his brother Athánatos fully and perfectly. He used to go out shooting, and when he came back he would take Athánatos on his lap and play with him.

We may now leave these people and look at the ogre who was terrified and wanted Johnnie to go away, that so he might live free from care. In the evening when he and his wife were in bed and Athánatos lying between them, and Johnnie in another room downstairs: 'O my queen,' said the ogre, 'How can we live in this way in such terror of your son?' 'And what can I do to help you?' said she. He said: 'There is nothing for it but to poison him, and so he won't be with us any more.' Athánatos pretended to be asleep, but his ears were all keen to hear what they were saying about his brother. The ogre said: 'When he comes back from hunting we will put the poison into the jar from which he drinks and washes himself.' Getting up in the morning, Athánatos hid himself and then went to find his brother. When Johnnie had eaten and drunk he went off hunting. The ogre and his wife put the poison into the water jar. Johnnie came back sweaty and tired, and his mother went to fetch the jar for him to wash himself. Athánatos went to tilt the jar, intending to spill the water, but Johnnie stopped him: 'You can't do this; you are too little.' The ogre heard Johnnie scolding the boy: 'Can't you let the boy do as he pleases, but go scolding him?' Athánatos stepping forward managed to tumble down and break the jar, and all the poison water was spilled. Johnnie took the boy in his arms saying: 'Don't scold the boy, but go and fetch some more water.' The two boys washed and drank and then sat down to eat.

In the night the ogre again said: 'Athánatos here is thwarting our plans; can he be hearing anything of what we say?' 'Oh no,' said she, 'he just lies there snoring. There is nothing left for it but we must soak the sheets in the poison, lay them on the bed and Johnnie shall sleep in them.' Athánatos was listening to all this. The pair started to do as they had planned. In the evening when Johnnie had come back from hunting and had had his supper, Athánatos took his book and sat down on the sofa. 'Come, my dear brother,' said he, 'and teach me my lesson, because in the morning my master will be beating me.' He opened his book and pointed at a whole string of lessons. 'All these, brother, I must learn by the morning, because if I don't I shall be kept in.' Said Johnnie: 'And I would rather teach you them myself; rather than you get into trouble.' They went on with their reading until it was dawn and never went to bed at all. Then Johnnie went away to his hunting. The ogre and his wife were very sadly vexed. 'For certain, yes, for certain, Athánatos was listening last night, for all his lying down to sleep.'

In the evening they again went to bed. The ogre said: 'There is nothing for it but that I change into a snake from the waist downwards with my upper part a man, and place myself above the window of the room. Then when Johnnie comes back from hunting, I shall wind myself round his neck and strangle him.' Said she: 'And this way will do very well.' But Athánatos was listening. In the morning when Johnnie rose up to go off, Athánatos said to him: 'You must take me with you.' 'But you are too small.' 'No, you must take me.' Well, Johnnie did not deny the boy, but got some little arrows ready for him and took him with him. They went on and on and so they came to the forest. Johnnie gave him his bow, and the child shot and killed birds, all as though he had been well practised. At home the ogre and his wife were very uneasy. What could Athánatos mean by going with his brother? The ogre turned into a snake from the waist downwards and curled himself up above the upper window and waited for the coming of the two boys. The way back was very long and Athánatos said to his brother: 'I am tired and you must take me up, my brother, and lay me on your shoulder; leave me there until we are at home, and then you can set me down on the sofa.' His brother took him up on his shoulders and they came to the outside door of the house, and there, when Athánatos saw his father turned into a snake, he gripped Johnnie's neck tightly with his arms, and so they went in. The ogre threatened him and shouted: 'Get down, you dog, get down: I'll eat you up.' But the more the ogre cried out, the more closely Johnnie was shielded by Athánatos's embrace. They went into the house, and the ogre refrained himself from Johnnie: otherwise he would have killed his own son. Then they stayed there eating and drinking.

When they lay down in the evening, the ogre said: 'This Athánatos, my dear wife, really ought to be killed. There is nothing else for it. I must go into the wood when they are asleep at midday and kill Johnnie, and then carry off my own son.'

There was a custom among these people that when a man chanced to be killed, he was laid on a pile of faggots and burned to ashes. So the ogre said: 'I will go to the boys, and when they see me they will kill me and then they will burn me. You must come and gather up my ashes and knead them into a paste, and Johnnie shall eat of the paste and that will kill him; never mind if I myself am no longer alive. And if my own son eat of the paste, it will do him no harm.' Athánatos was listening to all this. Dawn came and they got up. All the way the boy Athánatos was with Johnnie. As they were out shooting, at midday they lay down to sleep under a row of trees. Athánatos was on the look out. The ogre had started out and was now close to them. Athánatos said to him: 'What do you want coming here?' Then he gave Johnnie a push and woke him up. Then Johnnie seized the ogre and threw him to the ground and tore him to pieces. Athánatos, the son of the ogre, brought wood together and they burned the body. The ogre's wife saw that her husband did not come home, and seven sorrows were upon her. The boys came, and she could not but question them. 'O my mother, when we were shooting, an ogre appeared with intent to kill us, and we killed him.' 'Lucky you were, my sons, to escape from this danger.'

When they went out in the morning, their mother asked to go with them to take some comfort, because she was all alone; so she went with them. While the boys were shooting, she looked to find the ogre's ashes. She found them scattered here and there, and filled her bag with them, and then she went home to get food ready for the boys. For the most of the way Athánatos went with her; then he left her and she went on by herself. Then Athánatos sat down and told it all to his brother: 'Now, when we go to the house, beware of eating any of the paste. If you do I shall lose you.' They went home and the woman had ready two plates of paste. Athánatos took one of the plates and ate. Johnnie sat down, and she filled a plate for him. 'I am not eating, mother; I have no appetite.' She pressed him, and Johnnie took a morsel or two on a fork and said to her: 'If you want me to eat, mother, you must eat first.' Then, to make him eat, she took a mouthful. At once she fell down and died. Then the boys went off as their fate drew them.

After a long way they found a fork in the road. One of them said to the other: 'Now we must part.' Johnnie took the king's royal road; Athánatos followed the road of the vizier. Then they exchanged rings and Athánatos said: 'If my ring chafes your finger, then you must start out and look for me;

and if your ring chafes me, then I will come to you.' They kissed and went off.

Johnnie came to a town, to a royal palace, and the king was at war. 'My king, I have come to help you in the war.' He was put into the army, and the king was victorious. 'Now, my boy, I want to give you my daughter.' He prepared the wedding, and set the wedding crown upon Johnnie. Three days after he was married Johnnie saw in the room on the ground floor a closed window—it was never opened—and he opened it, and saw a road. He said to the queen: 'What road is this?' She said: 'The road with no return.' 'Well, good-bye,' said he. 'Where are you going?' said she. 'There is an ogre there who has a fair daughter, and whoever goes to woo her is killed by the ogre.' So Johnnie went to the place and found the ogre and said: 'I have come here to wrestle with you. Let us go to the threshing-floor of steel.' The ogre gave him a blow and killed him, driving him right into the earth. At that moment Athánatos was so much chafed by his ring that he was ready to cut off his hand; he left everything and went off to find his brother Johnnie. Then he presented himself before the king, and when the queen saw him, she said: 'Welcome here, Johnnie.' He said: 'No, I'm not Johnnie,' and he told her all the story, and then went on the same road as his brother. When Athánatos came to the place he saw the ogre's daughter and was amazed at her beauty. She said to him: 'Go away, young man, lest the ogre see you and kill you: I indeed have compassion on you.' 'And where is the ogre?' 'He is asleep,' and she told him where: 'and you may go and find him.' Athánatos went and woke up the ogre, saying: 'My ogre, I have come here for us to wrestle together.' The ogre took him to a room that was all full of weapons, and the boy chose a weapon all rusty—for so the ogre's daughter had instructed him—and girt it on: it then shone very brightly. Then the ogre said: 'I have here three threshing-floors: one is of lead and one is of steel and one is of iron. To which of them shall we go?' Said Athánatos: 'Let us go to all three.' They went to the floor of lead: they sank right into the ground. Then they went to the floor of steel; it broke under their weight. So they went off to the floor of iron. There they fought with their swords: neither of them won. Then they fought with their fists, and their fists smote like great clubs. Athánatos gave the ogre a blow and drove him into the ground, even up to the waist. 'My lad,' said the ogre, 'and what is your name?' 'Athánatos,' said he, 'he who knows not death.' 'That accounts for how you've conquered me.' Athánatos then gave him another blow and pushed him right down into the iron floor. There he left him and went off to find the daughter.

Then he questioned her: 'That last young man, the one who came before me: find him for me; I want him.' Then she went and raised up to life again all the youths who were lying there dead: Johnnie too she brought to life again and sent him off back to the queen.

Then Athánatos abode there and married the ogre's daughter, and they lived a life of very great good fortune.

7

The Wild Man and his Daughter

THE beginning and the end of this story from Nísyros present the theme of the daughter who fell into disfavour with her father because she dreamed that one day he would do her menial service when she washed her hands; he then drove her out. Finally she came to wealth and her father to poverty, and he unwittingly did her this service. So far we have the reverse of the first type of *The Boy's Dream*, a story discussed in *M.G.F.*, No. 53. But in the present story the seemingly presumptuous dream of the child and its triumphant fulfilment is no more than the frame, the beginning and ending, of the significant part of the story. What comes between is the story of the heroine and the kindly Wild Man, who adopted her when she was cast out by her own father, and was for so long jealous of her suitor, who was naturally his rival in the contest for the girl's love and devotion. The king, her lover, tried to win her over to his side and destroy her love for her father the Wild Man by means of the bird who acted as his spokesman. The Wild Man did what he could to keep her affection for himself, by making her believe that the bird was equally self-seeking, and this occurred the conventional three times until the bird was so much discouraged that he had lost all his feathers. The king then made a fresh move and sent his mother in correct form with gifts and proposals of marriage; this again the usual three times. By the Wild Man's advice the gifts were treated always with contumely; the fine chain used merely for hanging up the lamp, the bracelets as collars for the dogs, and the pearl thrown to the hens to peck at. Then the definitive gift was sent, the ring of betrothal. At this point the Wild Man changed his attitude and gave up the struggle to keep the girl for himself, for he knew that after all it is against nature that a girl should cleave to her father and reject a devoted suitor. So he told his daughter to accept her persistent lover.

The Wild Man's death is presented as the final expression of his desire for his daughter's happiness; he left her what seems to be in a figure the greatest of all treasures, the memory of a loving father. After her marriage the story reverts to what it began with, the girl's dream, and we see the father reduced to poverty coming to the court of his now wealthy daughter, and by serving her with a basin and water fulfilling the dream which had given him so much offence.

The rattling gourd which prevents the girl from perceiving that she has been left alone, occurs in other stories in similar situations. Sometimes it is a stone or an axe hanging up; anything to make a rattling noise as the wind shakes it.

Of this story there is a much inferior variant in *Dokímion t. gloss. idiómatos Karýstou*, by E. G. Papakhatzís, p. 97.

NO. 7. THE WILD MAN AND HIS DAUGHTER[1]

In those days there was a king and he had three daughters. The idea came to him to build for his daughters three palaces, and when he had finished them he took each one of the daughters to her own palace. Then he said to them: 'Now lie down to sleep and see what you will dream about me.' So the girls lay down to sleep. When God brought back the dawn, the eldest daughter rose up and went to her father. She bowed and kissed his hand in greeting, and then said: 'Good day, my father.' 'And a good day to you, my daughter. What did you dream about me last night?' 'I saw you, O my father, and you were in the midst of the sea sitting on a carpet all made of gold, and like the sun your face was shining brightly.' At this her father was well pleased and said: 'I can see, my daughter, that you love me well.' Then the second daughter came and she too kissed his hand. When she had greeted him, he asked her what she had dreamed about him. The girl said: 'I saw you in a ship and you were sitting on a chair of gold, and I took and filled your pipe for you to smoke.' Then came the third daughter; she greeted him, and he said to her: 'What did you dream about me?' The girl said: 'I, O my father, saw the moon and with it a star, and then, as the star was to wash her hands, the moon started to bow down in service before her. Well, my father, you may interpret the dream, for I cannot.' Her father was very much vexed and said: 'Can it ever be that you will be the ruler and I bow before you in service to wash your hands?'

[1] Text from Nísyros; printed in *Zographeíos Agón*, i. 421.

What then did the king do? Privily he called one of his servants and said to him: 'Take this my youngest daughter and carry her off fifteen hours away right into the mountains, and there leave her for the wild beasts to devour her.' What then did the servant do? He went and got ready two horses; then he went and said to the girl: 'Will you come with me, my princess? For your father has bought a fine garden and we may take a stroll in it.' The girl consented, for she did not know what was her father's intention. The two mounted and for fifteen hours went on their way until day was giving place to night. Then the servant said to the girl: 'If I leave you here, could you find your way back to the city?' The girl said: 'Of course; have I no eyes?' So the servant did not then dismount, but went on until the next day was dawning. Later he spoke to the girl again: 'Now, my princess, could you from here find your way back to the city?' The girl said: 'No; I cannot,' for indeed it was night. 'Stay here,' said the servant, 'and wait for me while I go and cut some wood, and then we can tie up a faggot of it and start back.' The girl said: 'And where is the garden you told me about?' The servant said: 'It is a long way from here. I wish now I hadn't brought you here.' Then he laid down a carpet for her underneath a tree and left some bread and food with her and so went off. He made up a bundle of wood and loaded the horse, and so went back home again. Before he went, he tied a dried gourd to a tree so that the wind kept the gourd rattling and the girl thought he was still there cutting wood. The girl waited until it was fully night; then she said: 'Can he be all this time cutting wood just to make a faggot? I must go and see.' She went and was aware that the noise she had heard was just the rattling of the gourd. She wept and lamented; she did not know what to do, for there she was on the mountain in terror of wild beasts, and of men too. She climbed up on a tree and took off her belt and tied herself with it so as not to fall down when she was asleep in the night. She was in this way up in the tree when the day dawned.

The girl came down from the tree wondering where she should go: what road she should take, for she now understood that her father had sent her away like this because of the dream she had told him. Then she was walking over the mountains and over the hills: maybe the wild beasts would devour her; maybe she might fall in with some men. So in a level place she saw in front of her something white. Said she: 'I must run and go up to that white thing to see what it can be.' So she came to it, and it was a tower. She saw the doors were open and she went in. When she came into the palace she saw meat there; lambs hanging up and roe deer. The girl was hungry and tired and there was no one there, so she said to herself: 'Whether I do this or whether I don't, it is anyhow all up with me. I must cook something to eat.' So she ate, and then she cleared the table and set it in order, and went and hid herself up in a lemon-tree in the garden, because she was afraid that the house might belong to some savage monster. At sunset she heard heavy footsteps and saw a Wild Man coming into the palace. He saw the table all set ready, and sat down and ate and drank and gave thanks, saying: 'What person can have done me this kindness?' The girl was afraid to show herself; she waited to secure a promise from the Wild Man, and then she would show herself. The Wild Man cried out: 'O you darling; light of my eyes; show yourself and I will do you no harm. If you are a man, I will make you king; if you are a girl, I will make you queen.' The girl was still afraid to show herself. The Wild Man rose up and ate and drank and then went back again to his hunting. The girl went into the palace and washed up everything. She set the house in order and cooked a meal and ate. Then she laid the table and hid herself again, in the same place. The Wild Man came and once more he saw the table laid and the house all in good order. The Wild Man began not to be willing to eat any more all by himself: rather he cried out: 'O thou light of my eyes, who are you who do me all these kindnesses?' Yet the girl could think of no way of presenting herself, and that night also she passed up in the lemon-tree. At dawn the Wild Man ate and went away. In the evening he returned and saw the same thing: he was not willing to eat all by himself, not unless the girl showed herself. Then he began crying out: 'O thou light of my eyes, show yourself to me. Do not be afraid; I will do you no harm.' Then he began to invoke with an oath the stars and the moon and the sky: 'If I do you any harm,' said he, 'may the sky burn me up!' When the girl heard this oath, she let herself be seen: the Wild Man was most delighted with her: 'Why, my dear girl, did you not show yourself yesterday, even the day before yesterday, and not put poor me to such torment? Sit down and let us eat and drink and from today know that I am as your father, and you I will know as my daughter.' When he had eaten, then he said: 'Where were you before? What brought you, who are such a fair princess, to come into these mountains?' The girl told him everything that had happened to her; all her sufferings.

So they fell asleep, and when God brought about the dawn, the Wild Man rose up and said to the girl: 'Now you stop here in the house and eat and amuse yourself, and don't be afraid because you are left alone.' So thus they passed two days, three, five days, the girl there all by herself. One day she said to the Wild Man: 'My father, how long must you go on hunting? Stay here at home for me to see you, and you see me, and I pass a day with you.' The Wild Man said: 'To give you pleasure I will stay.' So the Wild Man stayed there with her two or three days. As they were sitting there one day the girl told him all that had happened to her, and he what had happened to him. Then she said: 'Come, my father, and let me cleanse your head.' As she was cleansing his hair, she saw a piece of cloth tied on to his head. She said: 'What cloth is this, father? What is inside it?' 'These, my daughter, are the keys of my storehouses. Now that you have seen the keys, you may take them, and when I go away, you open the storehouses and take your pleasure in them, for in them are treasures of all sorts.' When the Wild Man had given her the keys and day dawned afresh, he went off to his hunting, saying to her, however: 'You see, my daughter, these forty storehouses: open them, but the last storehouse you may not open; if you do you will suffer for it.' So the Wild Man went off.

The girl then rose up to go to take her pleasure in the storehouses. She opened them all, but the last one she did not open: not until three days had passed. After three days she made up her mind and opened it. She looked at the storehouse: there was nothing in it. Then she saw that the storehouse was half lighted by a small window which stood a little open. She opened the window and through it she saw into a royal garden. From it a scented wind blew upon her, for there in the garden were trees of many kinds. She was glad to take her embroidery and sit there to her sewing. Then there came a bird all of gold; it perched upon a lemon-tree and said to the girl: 'Alas, for the girl; for her pride and for her beauty, all among the blossoming flowers! The Wild Man is feeding her and all to make her fat and to make her fair; then he will kill her and eat her up.' At this the girl was frightened and said to herself: 'So that is why he treats me well and brings me such food to eat; just to make me fat and then to eat me up.' The girl could no longer work happily at her embroidery and was full of sadness. In the evening the Wild Man came and saw her sorrowful, and said: 'What is the matter, my girl, that you are sorrowful? Can you have opened that storehouse? Tell me what you saw inside it.' The girl told him all that the bird had said to her. Then said the Wild Man: 'Oh no, my daughter. I had once a girl like you and a wife too; then from what the bird said to her my daughter met her death. But, my girl, you must not believe the bird, for he wants to bring you to your death and all for his own pleasure. But, see here: in spite of him you may go and sit there at ease, and when he comes to say to you the same thing again, then you must say: "Alas for the bird, for his pride and for his beauty, all among the blossoming flowers. The king is feeding him that he may kill him, and I, newly wedded, may eat his flesh when I am married to the prince; and that I, a newly wedded bride, may sleep on his feathers; and that his blood my father here may drink, all in a fine china cup." ' Then the bird took fright and flew off. From one of his wings the feathers dropped off. The king saw the bird with his feathers falling and said to the gardener: 'What is the matter with the bird that his feathers are falling?' And he told the gardener to watch and see who it was making the bird lose his feathers. Then the girl said to the bird the same words as she had said the first time: the bird again flew off and the feathers fell from the other wing. The gardener went and told the king. The king wanted to go and see the girl himself, and he went and kept watch by the lemon-tree. The girl and the bird came bickering together; the words all the same as before. When the bird heard the girl's song, he flew off, and from his tail all the feathers had dropped.

The king was afraid that something might happen to the girl, and he told his mother to go and make proposals for her hand, and she should take her as a present the king's chain. So the queen did as her son had told her. The Wild Man knew what was intended and he said to the girl: 'Tomorrow a proposal for your hand will come and you will be brought the man's chain. You must take it and fasten it to the wall and hang the lamp from it.' The girl did as her father told her.

When the queen saw that they were using the chain just to hang up the lamp, she was much vexed and went and told her son. He said to her: 'No matter. You go again tomorrow and take her your bracelets.' The girl's father, that is to say the Wild Man, said to her the evening before: 'When she brings the bracelets, you must call for the puppies and put the bracelets on their necks.' So the girl did as her father had told her. The queen was very much vexed and spoke to her son and told him that she would not go there with any more proposals. The king begged his mother to go on the following day also, and to take her as a present the pearl. Again her father told the girl to throw the pearl to the hens for them to peck at it. Again she did as the Wild Man had told her. The queen went back to the king and said that she would not go again on this errand. The king told her to go again on the next day and take the gifts of betrothal: then the girl would accept him. The Wild Man said to the girl: 'Tomorrow the queen will come and bring the gifts of betrothal; you must receive them with joy and bow and kiss her hand and put on the ring.' Next day the queen came and the girl did as her father the Wild Man had told her. High rejoicings were held and the pair put on the crowns of marriage.

Fifteen days later the Wild Man said to the girl: 'I have, my daughter, a very ugly habit of body. Epilepsy, the disease of the moon, seizes me and for an hour or two I lie on the ground writhing.' The Wild Man himself took and sharpened the axe and said to his daughter: 'When the fit seizes me, you must have ten lads under orders to keep watch, and when I am agonizing you must take the axe and cut off my head. And when you have cut off my head, you must grip my body and order the young men to set me in place. I shall be changed into a golden throne and on it you shall sit, and my head you must bury in the ground, and from it a tree will spring up which will cover with its branches all the field, and in the evening there will be upon it flowers like pearls, and in the morning they will be piled beneath it in heaps on the ground. Then you must send out a crier to proclaim to all the world that people may come and gather up the pearls, and wish you a long life and to me every blessing of rest.' As he bade her so the girl did.

From the time when the girl went away from her original father all his wealth and his prosperity left him. Then he learned that a queen had come who showed kindness and mercy to all the world, to poor and to rich. So he took his servants and went with a train of forty camels to the place where his daughter was. The girl was sitting at the window when she saw her father; she saw who it was and told her husband. So they came down and opened the gate and bowed down before him and kissed his hand. Then the girl set a great table and invited all the high lords and they sat down and ate. Then her father rose to his feet and took the water vessel for her to wash her hands. When the girl saw him do this, she fell down in a faint. Her father poured the water over her and brought her round from her faint and said: 'What is the matter with you, my princess?' The girl said: 'I saw in a dream that you would pour water over me for me to wash, and you drove me away into the mountains, and now here you are doing it all of yourself.' Then the king and his daughter knew one another, and she loaded up his forty camels, and he went off to his kingdom and there he stayed as when the story began.

8

Fair as the Sun

IN this story from Chios the heroine is promised by an old woman that her husband shall be a man called Fair as the Sun. So in a ship given her by her father she set out to find him. In every place to which she came she had herself sold as a slave. In the first country she saved her master from his wife, a horse-devouring monster, what the Greeks call a strigla; her reward was a gold ewer. In the next country she again freed a man from his wife, a corpse-eating ghoul, like Amine in the Arabian Nights; her reward was a gold coffee-pot. The third place she came to was where Fair as the Sun lived. Here the vizier's daughter had lost the power of speech; Fair as the Sun had given her a drug to prevent her from denouncing him. The heroine found out that he visited her at night. Over the window she hung a curtain which shut out the light entirely. In this way the pair did not know that day had come, and when the curtain was suddenly withdrawn, they were revealed together. Blackmailed by the heroine with the threat of exposure, the vizier's daughter gave in and left the field clear for her rival. Being no longer drugged by Fair as the Sun, she had recovered her speech, and the heroine was rewarded with a napkin of great price. With the ewer to wash his hands and with the napkin to wipe them and with coffee from the golden pot, the heroine served Fair as the Sun: he returned her love and they were happily married.

This story I find nowhere else. It is a kind of converse of the youth seeking to find the Fair One of the World, with whose supposedly hopeless love an old woman has cursed him when he angered her by breaking her pot or dish and then laughing at her.[1] In a story from Skyros we read of a curtain which prevents it being seen that the dawn has come. This is not altogether because of its thickness, but because it is also embroidered with the starry sky, so that a man, waking up in the morning, would believe that it was still night and that he was looking at the stars shining.[2]

[1] For details see *Forty-five Stories*, p. 346.

[2] See ibid., p. 389.

NO. 8. FAIR AS THE SUN[1]

A certain king made it a rule to drink always freshly drawn water, and that the water might be fresh he had them draw it from the spring at the moment when he wanted to drink. Also he would not drink any other water but what came from the spring outside his palace. For this purpose he had a gold cup of his own, and from this he used to drink, nor would he allow anyone else to drink from this cup of his.

One day his eldest daughter went to fill the cup, and as she was filling it an old woman appeared and begged her to give her to drink from that cup, to moisten her lips and to rejoice her heart. The girl refused to let her have it.

Another day, when the second sister went to fill the cup, the same old woman again appeared and asked to drink from it, and this second sister also refused.

Another day, the third daughter went to fill the cup, she who was the youngest, and the same old woman came and asked for water and to drink from the golden cup that her heart might rejoice. And the girl bethought her that it would do no harm to the cup if the old woman should drink water from it, and she gave it to her. 'O my daughter,' said the old woman, 'may you have my blessing, and it is given you from all my twenty fingers and toes; also may God grant you to have as your husband the man Fair as the Sun.' The girl took water to her father, and then she began to wonder who this man Fair as the Sun could be; and without knowing him she fell in love with him, and in time she began to look sad and sick.

This youngest daughter of his the king loved very heartily, because she was his youngest and the most beautiful, and when he saw that she had gone sick and become pale and yellow, he asked her one day: 'What is the matter, my daughter, that you are thus?'—'My father and king,' said she, 'what will please me and save my life is this: that you consent to let me have a ship that I may travel about the world to see countries and cities. Also, I should have with me forty young men, and my nurse to be to me as a mother.' The king loved

[1] Unpublished text from Chios recorded by Kanellakis.

her and would not thwart her wishes, so he got ready everything for which she asked him, and put her in a ship; at once she went her way to foreign lands. In the first to which she came a market was being held, and she told her nurse to bring her out of the ship and to put her up for sale for three thousand piastres. 'But, my daughter,' she asked, 'why this?'—'Do as I tell you, nursie, and time will make the reason plain.' The nurse went off and sold her for three thousand piastres, and the girl was bought by a man who kept a stable.

The first evening, like the princess she was, she could not sleep, and at midnight she saw the door opened where her master and mistress were sleeping. Then she saw her mistress coming out of the door and going downstairs. The girl thought that something secret was afoot and she ran after her to see where she would go; and, one, two, the lady went to the stable where the horses were, and one of them she disembowelled and started devouring it. And before she had finished, the girl had turned and gone back to the house; thus she learned the secret that her mistress was a strigla and devoured horses.

In the morning when her master rose up the girl found a means to talk to him, and said that if he would make her a present of a golden ewer enriched with precious stones such as not even the king could ever have, and if he would also give her her freedom, then she could tell him who it was stealing his horses.

When the master of the stable heard her he promised her what she asked of him, because for every horse lost he had to buy another, and the king know nothing about it; else he would have killed him. So the girl told him to try not to drink what his wife would give him when they lay down to sleep, but he must spill it out on his dress so that she might not notice. Then at midnight he must pretend to be asleep, and if he sees his wife get up to go away he must say nothing; she would speak to him herself and tell him what he must do.

All this the master of the stable did, and at midnight his wife disappeared. Then the girl called to him to get up quickly and follow her. She took him by the hand and brought him to the stable, and he saw his wife devouring a horse. Then they turned back quickly and came to his house and he pretended to be in a deep sleep. Then the girl too turned and went to her sleep. And in the morning, before the woman rose up, her husband took some very strong fellows; he went to the bed where his wife lay, and the men bound her. Then they took her off to the mountains and killed her. And thus he was delivered from a great and intolerable affliction.

After this he offered to take the girl as his wife, but she told him not to forget their bargain and the promises he had made. So he gave her the golden ewer all adorned with diamonds, and set her free as well. Then she ran down to her ship and went on board. Her nurse had been lamenting for her, and when she saw her she was filled with joy. 'Set the sails,' cried the girl, 'we must go off to another country.' They went off and continued their voyage until they came to another land; there they dropped anchor. Then once more she bade her nurse sell her for three thousand piastres and not a penny less. They went to the market and she was bought by one of the rich men, a great merchant.

In the evening at table she saw the merchant's wife, and wondered at her being so very stout and strong and her husband so feeble and as it were half dead, all skin and bones. When the work which she was ordered to do was finished, she went to lie down to sleep. But sleep did not come to her and she remained awake all night. Then at midnight she heard a voice and she pricked up her ears: 'Get up, for it is time.' Then she saw her mistress get up and go downstairs. She too got up and secretly followed to see where she would go. She observed that her mistress and five or six other women went into a shop; there they bought shovels and picks and went off to a cemetery. They opened a tomb and took out a corpse and sat down to devour it. When she saw this, she understood that all these were women who devour the dead. Before they had finished she turned back secretly and went to the house without anyone being aware of her. She did not go to bed because she wanted to see, when the woman came back from the grave, whether she would lie down to sleep, or was there anything else she would do?

When the man-eater came back she went to her husband's bed; she bent down and sucked at a wound which he had in his breast.

In the morning at dawn she called to her master and asked him why he was pale, so very pale and weak, and he told her that he had a wound from which he had suffered ever since he was married, and in spite of all his efforts to heal it, no remedy could be found. Then the girl told him that she could cure him if he promised to give her her freedom, and also to make her a vessel for making coffee all of gold and adorned with whatever in the world is rich and rare. When he heard this the merchant was delighted to promise her everything; he was a man of very great wealth.

Then the girl enjoined him not to drink what his wife gave him after they had eaten, but he must try to spill it as well as he could, and that his wife must not see that he had done this. This he must do three successive times, and the fourth time in the evening he must not go to sleep; the girl would call him to get up and take him where he could see with his own eyes what was going on. And when the three evenings were over, on the fourth evening when midnight came she woke him and took him off with her and let him see from afar off his wife and five or six others with her; they went into a shop and bought shovels and picks and before you could say Amen they went to a graveyard and dug up a tomb and pulled out a corpse and were devouring it. And all this the master saw with his eyes. And when he had very clearly seen it all, the girl took him off, and they went to the house, and she told him to pretend to be asleep when his wife came back from the graveyard, whatever she might do to him.

When the wife came back she ran to her husband's bed and bent down and sucked at the wound as we have already told.

In the early morning the master got up before she was awake, and he took some of his own men, strong fellows, and they went and tied the woman tightly to the tail of a horse; then they gave the horse a good hard cut with a stick, and it ran off so violently that she was at once dashed to pieces before you could say Amen.

The man, set free from such a great and mysterious plague, and she who had saved him being his young slave girl, asked her to be his wife, to make her lady and mistress of all his goods. But she asked for the things which he had promised and agreed to give her. Then seeing what she wanted and her insistence, he gave her the coffee pot, such as no one else had, and her freedom as well. At once she went off to her ship and ordered the men to set sail to yet another country. And when they arrived they at once furled the sails and dropped the anchor. After an hour she again said to her nurse that she must take her and sell her for three thousand piastres without dropping the price even a farthing.

Then she went to the mart, and all the men were eager for her, but the vizier bought her for three thousand piastres exactly and precisely; he paid so large a sum that his daughter might have her as a companion, because she was an only daughter and she was also dumb. When she had gone to the house and they came to know her well, she asked when the girl had lost her voice. The vizier said it was two or three years before that. Then one evening she began listening carefully: who was it talking in the room where the vizier's daughter was? She heard the girl speaking words of love and she heard also the name, Fair as the Sun. And when she heard this she strained her ears to listen again in case she had misheard, and again she heard the same thing and was sure that she was not making a mistake. At once her ancient grief and pain began to prick her, for the old woman's prayerful blessing had been that she should take Fair as the Sun for her husband.

So she took thought how she should begin and how she could manage such a piece of work. In the morning she went to the vizier, taking care that no one should see her, and very quietly she spoke in his ear: if his daughter wanted to have her power of speech, she could bring this about. In his delight the vizier wanted to kiss her to show how thankful he was; she drew away from him, saying that he was a vizier and ought to act in the lofty manner befitting his rank. At this he felt a check, and he asked her what present she would like. She asked him to cause a napkin to be embroidered for her, a web beyond price, and that he should give it to her, and her freedom as well. And the vizier at once faithfully promised her this.

'Well,' said the girl to him, 'since you want your daughter to be cured, you must send her away far from the palace into the country, and there rooms must be made ready for her in the manner I shall tell you.' So the daughter was sent out into the country. And then the girl told the vizier to order a curtain which he should hang up with great art in his daughter's window, in such a way that she herself without being seen could raise it, and the curtain should be so made that when it was lowered it should make it seem even by day as if it were the dead of night. He must also contrive a hiding-place where she could be hidden, and when she wished she could come easily and quickly to where the vizier's daughter was. The vizier did all these things as she had ordered him, and when he had finished and there was nothing left undone, he brought his daughter to the place.

Fair as the Sun, who was the prince of that land, heard that the vizier's daughter had come to the house. He again went very secretly in the evening and by the window he entered the house in his night clothes. He gave the vizier's daughter something to drink and she began to talk; then they began to sport and to behave in every way like lovers. But the girl who was concealed heard it all and artfully and skilfully she lowered the curtain, and so even when it was quite fully dawn the pair of lovers thought that it was still night, and played together heedlessly and freely. But suddenly the curtain drew up and it was plain that it was day. The pair of them were then as though out of their wits, utterly confounded. Fair as the Sun jumped out of the window like a bird and ran off to his palace. The draught that would have made the girl dumb was still in his pocket; he had forgotten to give it to her. Then when he had gone away out came the girl from her hiding-place and stood before the vizier's daughter; who, when she saw her, gave a loud cry. Then said the girl to her: 'You and I alone shall know the secret of what has happened. Fair as the Sun will not come here again, and I will tell everyone that you have been cured, and you to save your honour must keep silent.' All this the vizier's daughter understood very well; she consented, and called for her father. He came and the girl assured him that now his daughter had her speech as at the beginning and that she was no longer dumb.

When the vizier saw his daughter well he sought to take the strange lady and marry her, but she answered that he must remember his agreement with her and his promises. So he made no further objection, but set her free and gave her also the web embroidered with diamonds. When she had received it, she went to the ship and there she put on royal robes all decked with jewels; outside she wore a man's dress so that she should not be known. So, one, two, and off she went to the palace of Fair as the Sun and she asked the porter to let her go in to talk to the chamberlain, who was her kinsman; into his hand she slipped a big gold piece. Then she passed forward to the next man and to him she gave two pieces, and so to the third, and to him she gave twelve, and thus she succeeded in getting upstairs, and there she found the chamberlain. 'Come here, brother, I want to say something to you. In this world everyone has some fixed desire, a part of his nature. I have laid a wager that I will succeed if only for once in pouring out water for the king to wash himself. So I beg of you, if you please: today pretend to be sick and I as your kinswoman will take your place and pour out water for him to wash. If you are willing and consent to this, then I shall not lose my wager, and you may take these three hundred gold pieces which will be my profit from the wager.' For the sake of the money the chamberlain consented and took the gold pieces in advance, and so she presented herself with the ewer and the napkin and the coffee-pot, all three of them beyond price. Thus she poured out water for him. After what had happened in the night Fair as the Sun was almost dead: sad and depressed and his face cast down. He washed himself, and with such a ewer before him and such a coffee-pot and such a napkin and a strange servant as well, he did not know what was happening to him; what was going on.

After a long while he lifted up his eyes, and he was rapt

away with delight. The girl at once threw down everything; she ran out and went into a room and locked herself in. Then the prince leaped up like a deer to catch her. This he could not do, but with his eye to the keyhole he looked in and saw a girl: for beauty she was an angel. 'Who are you?' he asked; 'An angel or a demon?' She answered: 'I am a child of a king even as you are: I am no vizier's daughter for you to make me dumb. An old woman laid this blessing upon me when I gave her water to drink and refresh herself, praying that I should marry and that my husband should be Fair as the Sun, and without knowing who it was I fixed that name in my heart. The name scorched my heart, and to divert my yearning for my unknown love I asked leave of my father to go and travel to this place and that, nor did I know at all that you were Fair as the Sun and king of the land upon which I now tread. Now if you are willing to take me for your wife, well; but if you do not want me, then here locked up, without water and without bread, I shall remain till I die.' When he had rightly heard all this, he felt moved with compassion for her, and he swore to take her for his wife and to marry her. When she opened the door to him and he saw her, he was amazed at her beauty, for indeed it can in no way be described or pictured.

The two embarked together and went back to her lord and father that he should give them his blessing. Their wedding was celebrated and they lived like one soul in loving companionship.

9

Fiorendino, or the Forgotten Bride

THIS story is discussed and a version from Kos printed in *Forty-five Stories*, No. 44, and a summary with references is in *M.G.F.*, No. 49. The thread of the story is plain enough and from the names used—the hero is always called Fiorendino and the girl sometimes appears as Dolcetta—as well as for other reasons, it is fairly certain to have come to Greece from Italy. The magical flight, in which the fugitives are variously transformed, has been discussed in *Forty-five Stories*, p. 484.

The latter part of the story is always, at least in parts, versified, though the verses show no uniformity except in general purport. I have remarked in *M.G.F.*, p. 332, that a good many Greek stories are apt at moments of special tension to break into a simple form of verse. This is not entirely at random, and Burton's remarks on the use of rhymed clauses in the prose of the *Arabian Nights*—Burton's Library Ed., viii. 190—are here to the point. These melodious fragments—I paraphrase his remarks—are not due to whim or caprice, but are used in highly wrought situations, and their placing arises from a real appreciation of the story. A friend points out to me that the same thing is found in Shakespeare; the example he gives me is *Twelfth Night*, where, in non-comic scenes, 'prose dialogue turns into verse as the emotion is heightened'.

NO. 9. FIORENDINO, OR THE FORGOTTEN BRIDE[1]

There was once a king and he was sick. There came a prince and the king took him to his daughter: he had been told that his daughter should diet this man for forty days; after this the king should kill him and take his blood and with this anoint his face. The girl fell in love with the prince, and at the end

[1] Text from Mytilene; printed in Kretschmer, *Der heutige lesbische Dialekt*, p. 486.

of the forty days she took him and they went off together. Her father went in pursuit of the boy, but he could not catch him, nor his daughter either. Her mother who was a witch started out to overtake her; the girl turned round and saw her mother. Said she: 'My mother has come up with us. Now I will give you a buffet and turn you into a church; in it I will be a monk.' The queen caught up with them and asked: 'You haven't seen a girl, have you?' The answer was: 'Just now she passed this way.' The queen went into the church to see if she could catch the girl. Then what could the girl do? She gave the prince a buffet and turned him into a lake, and she turned into a duck. Her mother ran up to catch her. The duck shook her wings and so confused her mother's sight. Then the mother cursed her and said: 'He shall take you to his village; then his mother shall stoop down to kiss him and he shall forget you.'

They went to the prince's village. The prince took her to an old woman's cottage and said to her: 'You stay here, and I will go to my mother, and then the escort of musicians will come here to fetch you.' Said she: 'When you go to your mother, I beg of you that your mother shall not kiss you, for if she does, then you will forget me.' He went to his mother, and when she saw him she went mad for joy. 'O my son, what a loss you were to me! Come, let me kiss you.' 'Oh no, you must not kiss me; if you do, I shall forget my wife. Bid that men with their instruments of music go from here to take my wife from the old woman's house and bring her here. Now I must rest a little until the people have come.' He lay down, and sleep came upon him. His mother went and kissed him: he forgot his wife. Then his mother said: 'Get up, my son, and go and bring your wife here.' 'Why are the instruments of music playing outside the house?' His mother said: 'What are you talking about? You want your wife; now is the time to go to fetch her.' Said he: 'I have no wife.'

His wife was staying in the old woman's cottage. What then did she do? She went and set up house outside his father's palace. The staircase of the girl's house was finer than all the king's palace. The king's men woke up in the morning and they saw a great palace opposite their house, and in it a girl fair as the sun and with her three servants. 'Wake up, my son,' said the king. 'You must look at the palace over against ours; in it is a girl with servants waiting on her.' The young man got up and saw the girl; he did not recognize her; he had forgotten her.

He went to the tavern and there he talked to one fellow and then to another: 'There is a girl here you must come and see; maybe she will open her door to you and you can go in and take your pleasure.' One fellow went; he had tied up a hundred piastres in his kerchief and threw it in at the window. The servants took him and brought him to the lady. She said: 'Open the door and bring him in.' They brought him into the house and there they beat him; then they took and threw him out again. The prince went to another fellow and said: 'Now you go.' He tied up two hundred piastres in his kerchief and went and threw it in at the window. The servants brought him in to the lady. 'Bring him in,' said she, 'give him a dose and throw him out again.'

After their beating the two fellows went back to the tavern. The prince, who had thus forgotten his wife, questioned them: 'Where have you been?' he said. They said: 'We went to the house of the lady, our neighbour.' Said he: 'And I too must go there.' He tied up five hundred piastres in his kerchief and threw it in at the window. The girl said: 'Bring him into the house; give him a good dose and throw him out.'

The young man could not walk; there he lay outside the king's house groaning all night. Then said his father: 'Who is it there groaning all night?' He was told: 'It is your son.' 'Bring him in.' They took and lifted him up and carried him into the palace. They sent and summoned the woman and asked her why she had beaten the king's son. Priests had come to the palace; Turks too and great lords as well. The woman was there and greeted them thus:

A welcome fair to all the lords;
A curtsey to the priest;
Salam aleikum to the Turks;
Boys, welcome to the feast.

[Then one of the fellows from the tavern sang:][1]

I paid a hundred pieces;
  Two hundred pieces he;
And from the hapless Fiorendin
  Five hundred was your fee.

[Then the woman sang:]

Dost thou remember, O my love,
  How thou didst dwell with me?
Every fair scent was in that bed
  Where thou didst lie with me.

Dost thou remember, O my love,
  Hast thou forgotten me?
How thou wast like a holy church,
  And there I worshipped thee?

Dost thou remember, O my love,
  Hast thou forgotten me?
When thou wast like a lake so fair,
  Did I not swim in thee?

Then Fiorendino knew that she was his wife and they celebrated their marriage.

[1] For the sake of clearness I have inserted these sentences in brackets.

10

The Blessing Incarnate

THE value and power of the parental blessing is a recurrent theme in these stories, though of its incarnation in the form of a horse, an admonitory and prudent horse, I know of no other example; the helpful horse is of course a well-known figure. The general lines of this story from Chios are largely those of *The Son of the Hunter*, printed in *M.G.F.*, No. 42. In both stories we have the jealous vizier who tries to get rid of the hero by having the king send him on dangerous quests: and of the quests the killing of the elephants for their ivory is practically the same as the killing by the hero of the present story of the bird, whose bones are of pearl. In both stories the third and last quest is for a beautiful girl, whom the now elderly king is so foolish as to wish to marry. In an oven of rejuvenation she makes the hero even more handsome than before; then, inducing the king and the wicked vizier to enter it with the hope of being made young again, she turns them into a hound and a hare, thus punishing the king's folly and the vizier's wickedness.

The name of the girl, Dartané, is clearly the same as the Tartána of the *Forty-five Stories*, p. 346: it means a woman of slow movements and plump.

The way in which the hero ingratiates himself with the Lamia ogress is common in these stories. The ogress who would otherwise have devoured the hero is appeased by being addressed as 'Mother'. As a rule he demonstrates his filial feelings by sucking her breasts.

NO. 10. THE BLESSING INCARNATE[1]

Once there was a king and he had a son, his only child. The king loved this child very much and never thwarted his wishes: whatever the boy asked was done and this by the king's orders.

One day the boy said: 'I beg you, my royal father, before

[1] Unpublished text from Chios, recorded by Kanellakis.

I come to the throne to give me a frigate that I too may go and see manners and ways of life and learn how the world is governed.' 'My son,' said the king, 'great is my desire to please you, but both I and your mother are afraid that you may suffer from the sea; you are not accustomed to it.' But the boy insisted on his wish being carried out, and so the king told him to make his choice of a ship or frigate, whatever he wanted. The boy chose the finest of the frigates and put in her the choicest victuals and twelve young fellows, men who knew where to go and where not to go. 'Give me, my royal father, your blessing on my going away.' His parents heartily gave him their full blessing, and so the sailors took the prince and carried him to many places; he had a very fine voyage.

After a long time there came a newspaper reporting that the town where his parents lived had been sunk in a gulf; as they were being swallowed up in the gulf his father and mother had cried out: 'O my son, may our blessing, and that from all our twenty fingers and toes, be upon you wherever you may be.'

The prince heard the news of the engulfing of the town, and not long afterwards all his provisions came to an end and he no longer had any money. Then he said to the young men: 'My lads, you must find a vessel to go wherever you have a mind because I am going to sell the frigate.' And when he had sold her, then like a young man who had been brought up as he had been to live as a prince, he went on eating and drinking until all his money was spent. And when it came to an end he found a sailing vessel and said to the captain: 'Can you take me to the place where the disaster was, that I may go and see what has happened to my parents?' And when they had struck a bargain, he embarked on this ship and went off. The place which had been swallowed up was now all sea, and he started searching about here and there until at last he found the place where his house had been. So as a probe he thrust down a long pole, and as he was probing he heard a voice: 'Be very careful; look out that you do not hit me; you must be very careful how you bring me up.' And when the boy heard the voice he thought it was his father and his mother and took great pains to try to bring them up safely. But instead of his father and his mother he brought up a horse—he was of pure gold—and the horse spoke and said to him: 'Let the men go away, and you mount me and let us go out on the dry land, for I am the blessing of your mother and your father.' And so the prince mounted on the horse, and they came out upon the dry land and went off to find some dwelling of men; night and day they travelled until they should come to a city.

One evening something bright appeared before the prince, and when the horse saw this brightness he started to go faster, but the prince told him to stay still for him to dismount to see what it was. And the horse told him not to dismount; also to be careful not to pick up anything. But the boy dismounted and saw a bird's feather—it was beyond price—and he took it and showed it to the horse. And the horse said: 'I told you not to take it, but now that you have, may what will follow be to your good.'

Then again the prince saw another brightness, and when he saw it he halted the horse to dismount. He dismounted and found a girdle—it was beyond price—and he showed it to the horse. When the horse saw it he said to the prince: 'May what will follow be to your good.'

They went on their way for two more days and nights, and so they came to a city. And when they came outside the gate, they took thought to find a house to rent in which they could live, and thus look about and see what in the end they should do.

When they had taken a house and settled in it, the prince said to the horse: 'What now will become of us, for we have not what we need for our livelihood? I have thought to take the golden feather and to go to sell it to the king of the land.' The horse's advice was to sell it to the first customer who came their way.

The prince took the feather and went to sell it to the king; as he was going up the palace steps the vizier was coming down. And when he saw the boy going up, he asked him where he was going, and the boy answered that he was going to the king to sell him a golden feather. Then the vizier thought to buy it and made an offer of five thousand piastres, but the boy refused him even if he were to offer ten thousand, because he intended to sell it to no one but to the king. So he went into the king's presence and offered him the feather, and when he had looked well at it the king was struck with wonder: there was no price at which the feather could be priced. Then he clapped his hands and the vizier came before him, for without the vizier the king never made any decision. So he said to the vizier: 'This feather the boy here has brought me, and I have called for you to look at it that you may say at what price you would value it, that I may pay him for it.' 'Well,' said the vizier, 'whatever it may be, it is just a feather, and you may put your hand into your pocket and whatever you find, give it to him as payment.' So the king put his hand into his pocket and found five gold pieces. Then he asked the vizier: 'Is not this too little?' The vizier answered: 'Indeed it is a great deal to give for a feather, and all the more because no one knows where the boy got it.' The prince took the gold pieces and went off to see his horse, and the horse said to him: 'Did I not tell you whoever made you the first offer, to him you should sell it? You have no cause to be aggrieved.'

In a fortnight's time their money again came to an end; for a prince's money is very quickly spent. Then he said to the horse: 'I shall go and sell the girdle.' Again the horse's advice was that the boy should sell it to the first man he met who wanted to buy it. As the boy was going up the stairs of the royal palace the vizier was coming down, and when he saw the boy he asked him why he was going up. The boy said that he was going there to sell a girdle, and he showed it to him. And when the vizier saw it he wanted to buy it, and was ready to give him twenty thousand piastres. But the boy answered that even if he offered him forty, it was his intention to sell it to the king and to no one else. So he brought it to the king. And when the king took it and looked at it, he put it on his knee and saw clearly that for this girdle there was no price at which it could be priced. And he clapped his hands and the vizier appeared. The king asked him what was the price which he ought to pay. The vizier answered by saying that the thing was a girdle and nothing more, and that the king should put his hand into his pocket and whatever he found there he should give the boy as payment. So the king searched in his pocket and brought out five more gold pieces and gave them to the boy. Then the boy said: 'Surely five pieces are very little?' The vizier answered that they were in fact a great deal, and he told the boy to take the money and go away. When the boy heard these unjust words, he went off with tears in his eyes and went to see his horse. And when the horse heard what had happened, he said: 'Why did you not follow the advice I gave you? And now you sit weeping and weeping? You may well weep, seeing what will come to you later on.'

When the boy had gone the king took the feather and hung it up on one side of the room, and on the other side the girdle, and they shone there brightly, as when the sun is shining at full midday. Later on he called for the vizier and said to him: 'Come and see how brightly they are shining.' The vizier answered: 'Even with a feather and a girdle the room is shining brightly indeed, but, O, what would it be like if you had here the bones of that bird, each and all of which are of mother of pearl, and its wings which are of gold!' 'Well, and where can we find this bird?' Then said the vizier: 'The man who brought you the girdle and the feather, he is the man who can fetch you the bird as well.' So when the king heard what the vizier said, he summoned the boy and said to him: 'You are the right man to bring me the bird, whose bones are of mother of pearl, and its wings of gold, and I want you to bring these things without more ado.'

So the prince went off with tears in his eyes, and he went to the horse to tell of this last demand. Then he questioned the horse: 'I came upon the feather and the girdle; but the bird, in what manner can I come upon it?' The horse answered: 'Whoever acts disobediently and disregards the counsel of those who truly wish him well, following his own notions, all these troubles he must endure. But now, since this is the king's command, mount on me willy nilly and we will go and seek for the bird.'

So the youth mounted, and when he had come out from the town and had come to the mountains, there met him the Lamia, the ogress. He said to her: 'Welcome, my little mother; yesterday and the day before that we were playing together like as though I were a baby; now, alas! you are like the withered nut in its shell all rattling about.' 'Boy, boy, my boy, like a king you have honoured me and like a king you have spoken to me: if you had not done this, I would have devoured you. Where are you going this way?' 'I am going to find the golden bird.' 'And do you know where it is to be found? The bird is of very high spirit, and if it is to be caught it is not caught easily. Yet I will tell you what you must do. Over yonder there is a lake, and to it the bird comes down every midday, to three plane-trees which stand on the margin of the lake; then it goes to the lake and drinks, and as it drinks it sings, and all the place shines brightly, the mountains and the plain. Then when you go eagerly in pursuit of it, you must take with you twenty skins of raki and twenty of wine and also twenty strong lads; each of them must carry a well-sharpened axe, and when you have got all these things ready, you must turn and go to the lake and empty it and scour it out and pour in the raki and the wine. When you have done this and before midday comes you must all hide yourselves. At that very moment the bird will come down to drink. Then before it is fully aware that all the lake is raki and wine, it will get drunk; then you must all of you fall upon it and cut it to pieces, because if you try to take it alive, it will devour you all.'

So the boy took the horse and turned back and went to the king and asked him for all the things which the Lamia had told him; also with the condition that the vizier should bear all the expense. This was the advice given him by the horse, so that the king should not be allowed to put the prince under any obligation to him in the matter of expenses. The boy therefore asked that everything should be to the account of the vizier.

The king therefore summoned the vizier and said: 'Sir Vizier, you must get ready at your own expense forty skins of wine and raki and forty strong young fellows and as many horses, because they will all be needed for fetching the golden bird.' The vizier sent out the finest of the heralds and he made proclamation: 'Whoever is of manly strength, he must come to the king,' and so all the young men were brought together, and the prince took them. They set out and went very quickly indeed to arrive well before midday, and so they had time to open a channel from the lake by which they emptied it. They scoured it out well and poured in the raki and wine and then they hid themselves as the Lamia had told them.

At full midday there was a shining on the mountains and a shining on the fields; this was because the bird had come. At once it plunged into the lake and drank, and before it was well aware that it was all raki and wine and knew what was and what was not, it had drunk its fill. Then at once the bird lost its senses and fell down drunk in the sunshine, no longer conscious of anything. Then they all attacked it with their cutting axes and hewed it to pieces and brought all to the king.

The king called for his vizier and showed him the bird, and the vizier said: 'You see that the youth knew where the bird was.' 'What shall I give him?' asked the king. 'Nothing at all,' said the vizier, 'because on his horse he went and on his horse he came back; what did the boy himself do? To say nothing of the youths whom he had with him and the expenses which I had to pay.' The unfortunate prince went off without any reward.

The bones of the bird were all of mother of pearl and its feathers were all of gold, and when the king had made sure that this was so he gave his orders, and with the bones he had a room built and with the feathers it was overlaid. And when after forty days the room was finished, it was all shining brightly. Also he put the girdle there, and it shone like the sun. Then he sent for the vizier for him to see the room and to admire it. And when he had turned to the right and to the left and walked over the whole place, the vizier said to the king: 'It is indeed very fine, my lord and king, but how great you would be if you had for your own Dartané, she who is the Fair One of the World. He whose she is becomes in her arms a young lad of twelve years. Ah, what would you then be!' 'Well, and where is that girl to be found?' 'The man who brought you the feather and the girdle and the bird, he can bring you also the Fair One of the World.' The king sent for the boy and ordered him to bring him the beautiful

Dartané, the Fair One of the World. 'And where can I find her, my lord king?' 'Where you found the other things you have brought me, there you can find her also.' The prince went away to his horse and told him of the king's fresh demand, and again he mounted on the poor horse and they went off at random a long, long way.

As they were going on and on the Lamia met them. 'Good day to you, my good little mother. Yesterday and the day before we were playing together like mother and baby, and are you now, alas! so shrunk and wrinkled?' 'Ah, my boy, my boy, a royal lad, and you have given me royal honours; if not, I would have devoured you. Where are you going on this road?' 'I am on my way to find the beautiful Dartané, the Fair One of the World; do you know where she is to be found?' 'Alas, alas for you if you are in search of her! She has been now for forty days weeping aloud for the slaying of her brother, the bird. And can you be going to that place, all without help? Ten princesses are being held as slaves and they are all of them in rags; you must now go back and get ten royal dresses, and each dress must be a thing by itself, with its adornments and jewels, a thing apart from all others, and each dress separately you must pack into a bundle. Also you must make an iron ladder with forty steps fastened with screws, and when you have got all these things ready you must go and pass by the plane-trees and the lake, and there you will find the castle, inside which is the Fair One of the World. You must wait for a moment when you do not hear a sound, and then you must plant the ladder and go up on the castle, and all the girls will run to see who you are, because at that hour she whom you seek will be asleep, and they will be keeping the flies off her. For it is forty days since she has had any sleep, and all because of the killing of her brother the bird. And when you come there and go up into the castle, the princesses will ask you: "What do you want? Go away at once." But you must ask for nothing else but only for the pipe which she keeps by her pillow. And when they give it to you and you go down and are well away from the castle, then you must blow on the pipe, and the castle will be shaken and set in motion; nay, it will begin to stir and to move forward in obedience to the sound of the pipe.'

When the boy heard and understood all that we have been telling you, he turned back and went to the king and asked him for all the things which the Lamia had prescribed, the ladder with its screws and the ten dresses, all with their adornments and jewels, and all the expense to be at the cost of the vizier, because if the king spent even the smallest sum, he would not be bringing him as a sheer gift the beautiful Dartané.

So the king called for the vizier and ordered him that at once and without any delay and at his own expense everything must be provided for which the prince had asked. And the vizier, willy nilly and whether he had the money or hadn't—anyhow, he put all his goods in pawn and made the dresses and the ladder. And the prince took them and went to the castle and gave them to the princesses as the Lamia had bidden him. The princesses, not knowing what was going to happen, gave him the pipe for which he had asked, and when he was a long way off the castle he blew upon it, and the castle began to shake and to move and to go forward of itself at the sound of the pipe.

However deeply the Fair One of the World was sunk in sleep, when the castle began to shake and to move she woke up. She asked the girls: 'What is this which you have done to me?' And even before they had time to answer her, she caught at them one by one and drove them away. She pitched them all out of the castle, and they were killed. Then she threw out of the house everything else near her, and so the castle was left with nothing but four bare walls.

When the castle began to shift and to move, the prince ran forward quickly to the king and asked him where he should bring the castle to a stop, the castle which had in it the Fair One of the World. And the king ordered him to bring it to a stop close to his palace. When the castle came to a stop, the king asked to go up into it, that he might see the Fair One of the World. But she refused to receive him, and indeed she would not consent even to put her head out of the window, but told him that he must first gather up all the things which she had thrown out of the castle. The king might not thwart her wishes, and he commanded as many men as were needed to go and fetch mules to gather the things up and load the mules with them: all the things which she had scattered about. All this should be at the expense of the vizier. All this was done, and more especially they gave burial to the princesses, for they had all been killed when the Fair One had thrown them out of the castle.

When they had gathered up all that the Fair One of the World had told them, and had brought everything to the castle, they asked her if anything was missing, and she said: 'No; nothing but this only.' When she had been a little girl seven years old she had been put in a boat and taken for a cruise, and as she was sitting in the boat she had dipped her hand into the sea and stirred up the water, and as she was stirring the water her ring had fallen off: now the man who had brought her to the palace must fetch it from the sea for her.

When this command of the Fair One of the World came to the ears of the prince, for the king had summoned him and told him that he must go and fetch it out of the sea, he wept and groaned, but it was a royal command and he had to obey. So the prince went and told this to the horse, and the horse said that this would be his death, and the prince would lose him for ever. After saying this he told him also the story of the ring: this ring had fallen into the sea, and as it was falling it happened that the Jinn of the sea had swallowed it, and the moment it was swallowed the Jinn of the sea had become with child and had conceived a colt and to the tail of this colt the ring was tied: 'Well, you must go and make two iron corslets, the one to fit a horse and the other to fit a man; and the horse corslet I shall put on since I am a horse, and you must put on the man's corslet; then you must buy also a fine sword and all the costs must be on the vizier, even to the last farthing.'

The prince did all that the horse told him, and the king ordered the vizier to have the iron corslets made and the sword also, and when they were finished the prince took them. Then the horse told him that they should go to the margin of the sea and there they would find a cypress-tree, and at the foot of the cypress there was a spring, and there he must tie up the horse. The prince must climb up on the cypress, and when he had gone up the horse would begin to neigh loud and fast, and when the Jinn who was in foal in the midst of the sea heard it, then she would begin to neigh, and at last she would get angry, and from the greatness of her anger she would come out on the dry land and fall upon the boy's horse and the two begin to fight; and when they were fighting he would get a good chance to slit up the belly of the Jinn with the sword, and then the foal would leap out and on its tail would be the ring, tied there: 'and you must at once mount on him and grip him firmly by the mane and wind it round your hand and give him a stroke, and so you will be off like a bird.'

All of this the prince with great skill succeeded in doing, and when the foal issued from the body of the Jinn he leaped upon him, and the foal understood that he had to deal with a noble youth, and he said that he had a desire for such a rider, and that it was for this reason that he had chosen not to be born until that moment.

As soon as the prince had mounted the foal his own horse died, and when he had made sure that he was dead he sought to carry him off with him, dead as he was, because this horse was the Blessing of his Mother and of his Father. And when he came to the castle where the beautiful Dartané was, he called to her to come down to take the ring: it was tied on the foal's tail. She came down and took it. Then she ordered the men to heat the oven with big logs, and as soon as they had put in abundance of fire, she ordered them to cast the prince into the oven and his horse with him; then she sealed it up. When it was dawn she ordered them to break the seals and to collect the ashes, and then to celebrate her wedding to the king.

Very early in the morning those who had received the order went and opened the oven, and instead of finding the prince and his horse burned to ashes, they found them alive, and indeed the prince looked so handsome that the very best painter could in no way have depicted him, and all this was the dealing of God, because with the youth was the Blessing of his Mother and of his Father.

When the Fair One of the World saw all this she told the king to have the oven fired again and that he should go into it with the vizier, 'and when you come out of it, you will be like the boy, even handsomer than you now are, and then for sure we shall celebrate our marriage.'

The king was very old, and like an old man he was very ready to do what the Fair One had told him. So he ordered the oven to be fired and went into it with the vizier; then the men who had been ordered to do so sealed it up. In the morning they went and opened the oven, but instead of the king coming out looking more handsome than before as they had expected, they found that he had been turned into a harrier and the vizier into a hare. The two of them leaped out and took to the valleys and hills, the hound chasing the hare, saying: 'Why did you not let me show my thanks to the boy as I ought to have done for all those many good things he brought me?' And the hare answered: 'And why did not you act as king and master of the house as you were, and in accordance with justice and your duty, but instead listened to me who was your servant?'

After all this the Fair One of the World said: 'He who has succeeded in all these tasks, he shall be my husband and master of my life, so prepare the wedding that I may make him my husband. Set in order instruments of music; cook food; send out invitations to all the world, and tell the story of what has happened, to me and to him and to the king, who was so foolish as to desire another marriage, and that with a young girl; so doing injustice both to a young man and to a young woman. He was no good judge in these matters, a man unable to be warned by the passage of the years; nor did he know what the word parent means; nor what is the power of the blessing of a father, when the prayer comes from the very depth of the heart; how this blessing is for salvation; how it is a well of life, of honour, and of wealth, and the very strength of a man's hand.'

11

The Boy carried away to the World Below

OF this story from Naxos I know of no other versions. It has a certain narrative skill, though the dialogue between the wizards and the boy would be easier for a hearer than for a reader; I have smoothed away a few ambiguities. The thread of the story is, however, plain enough. A jealous rival set magic to work, and the bridegroom was caused to lose his way and passing down a long flight of stairs found himself in the World Below. Equally by magic art he escaped, and by means of his ring was recognized by his lady, with the usual happy ending. The way in which the denouement is brought about, the hero telling his adventures in the guise of a story, is a common device, for which see in particular *M.G.F.*, No. 57.

It may be asked why the good wizards of the World Below turned the hero into a blackamoor. These stories require not only that the virtuous shall be rewarded but that the wicked shall be punished, and for the punishment of the wicked wizard it was essential that he should not recognize the boy who brought him the letter, the letter charged with such magic that when it was opened it caused his house to fall down upon him. And this is of course why the boy was warned that he must on no account make any stay in the wizard's house.

This World Below occurs in a great number of Greek folktales. It seems to be a kind of fairyland tucked away out of sight, and only reached through some sort of suspension of voluntary action. It is never the world of the dead: in a story from Astypálaia[1] we are told very clearly that the people there are all alive. Here is not the place for more details; I have written a long paper on the subject which is now being printed in Greece.[2]

[1] The relevant passage is in Dieterich, *Sprache und Volksüberlieferungen d. Südl. Sporaden*, p. 508, l. 185.

[2] The paper, *The World Below in Greek Folktales*, is in *'Επ. ἑτ. βυζ. σπουδῶν*, xxiii, p. 312.

NO. 11. THE BOY CARRIED AWAY TO THE WORLD BELOW[1]

There was once a boy who had lost his mother; also he was an only child, but for making good progress there was no one to match him. Every year he would come out after the examinations with a face of better cheer than all the others, and always he would carry off the prize. All day he would sit at his books. They had made him a room to himself, and there he would go to the window and sit reading all day. Opposite was the king's palace, and the princess found her pleasure day and night in sitting with her lamp reading: this was not for a week or two but all the time. One day the princess called out to her nurse: 'Come here and look; don't you love to see that poor boy, who never fails to have a book in his hands?' 'And I too watch him all day; may it be a joy to him and a grief never!' 'Up then, and go and call my mother.' The nurse went off and called for the queen; she came and looked at the boy and said: 'May all this be to him a joy!' So the queen was going continually to look at the boy, as he sat there every day with the book in his hand. After a day or two the queen said to the king—everyone also was taking pleasure in the sight—'May joy befall the mother who has such a son! At his age boys, all of them, go playing in the streets and at night are all over the place amusing themselves, but this boy is day and night deep in the study of his books.'

Then the princess found an opportunity and said: 'I want him for my husband.' 'Very well, my daughter.' The king sent and told the boy's father that he wanted him to come to the palace. The poor fellow at once thought that the king would have his head and this was an order: yet what could he do? He went up to the palace. The king said to him: 'I want your son for my daughter's husband.' When the poor fellow heard such a proposal he said: 'My son is but a poor man. What can I have to say about such a matter?' When he saw for sure that the king was saying this seriously, he went and fetched his son, and he and the princess were betrothed. All day the boy was in the palace; they dressed

[1] Text from Naxos, printed in *Neoellinikà Anàlekta*, ii. 53.

him in royal clothes; also they made things ready for the wedding.

Now the princess had with her not only the boy but also a palace official, and this man was in love with her. Well, he grew jealous of the poor boy and went off to a wizard and prepared charms against the boy, so that he should be as dust scattered before the wind: nothing left of him. Then on the day of the wedding, when all the priests had been sent for, the boy went aside for a moment. Then he couldn't find the way out; all he could find were some steps which led downwards. He went down them, and down and down, some thousand steps and more, and so he came to a great palace. He walked all over it, and through the door he came out into a garden. Then he found himself in a town, but he could not see any steps or anything else by which to go back. Meanwhile the king was waiting for the boy, and so were the princess and the priests, thinking he would come out. Midday came but nothing happened. They went to look for the boy, but he was nowhere; nowhere at all. The wedding came to nothing and the guests all went away. But what joy for the official who now could marry the princess at once! But, lo, she refused even to look at him, and for the boy who had disappeared in this way she put on mourning, and in her grief would never go outside the palace: she made up her mind to remain for ever unmarried.

Now let us turn to look at the boy who was in that town walking about; it seemed to him a strange place. He was there for five or six days, and when he began to be hungry he would buy something and eat it just as he was, standing up; he slept in the open field. When his money had come to an end and he saw clearly that it was his fate to remain there, he took a post with a merchant as a serving boy; in this way he could earn his bread and have somewhere to sleep.

After two or three months he met three wizards, and they said to him: 'How is it that you are here?' The boy began his story from the beginning: 'A princess wanted to marry me, and on the very day of the wedding I went aside and could not find the door out, and then I went down some steps and so I came here.' 'Oh, my lad, they worked some magic on you. Here where we are is the World Below, and no chance that you can ever find your own land again. But now since we also are wizards, we can little by little bring you in three year's time to a sight of your own country. Meanwhile you must every morning take one of these powders.' Every morning the boy took a powder, one by one, all the time becoming blacker and blacker; in three years time he had become a regular blackamoor. Then the wizards went to him where he was in the merchant's house and said: 'Take this letter and go to the wizard, the one who in your own country worked that magic upon you'—for they knew that magic had been worked upon the boy—'and when you are with him, give him this letter and say: "Here is a letter from your friend So-and-so." He will ask you where you have come from: "Stop a while here with me," he will say. But no, you must not stay with him at all. And here too are letters which you must give to the king, and you are to make him understand that you are a native of this land here, the World Below, and that your father here in the World Below has given you letters for you to take to him, in order that they may become acquainted with one another. You must say that you will be stopping for some few days, and that then you will go back to your father. Then you will be taken into the palace to stay. And look: here is this ointment; as you rub yourself with it you will become as white as you were before.' When the wizards had given him these instructions, they went away.

Presently, when he had gone aside for a moment, he again could not find the door to go out, and again he saw a long flight of steps. He went up and up for a thousand steps and more, and so he came out on a flat plain all covered with trees and rivulets of water: then he saw the sea with some ten ships all with their sails set. He went down to the shore and there he saw a crowd of sailors. They said to him: 'Sir, we have been waiting for you to carry you to your own country.' He went into a ship and the other ships set sail all in company. When they entered the harbour of the boy's own country, they hoisted their flags: Bam, Boum; a salute of guns. The king, and this was the man in the house opposite to his, the man who was to have been his father-in-law, understood from this that some king had come to him. He sent men to the ships to welcome them. At once the boy disembarked and went to the palace, and handed over his letters to the king: letters to say that the king of the Blacks sent his greetings and that the boy was the son of that king and that in a few days he would be going away again. Then they stayed there in the palace; the people could hardly think what banquets and what ceremonies it would be fitting to offer him.

In the evening the boy went to the house of the wizard; he found him and gave him the letter, saying: 'Take this letter; it is from your very dear friend So-and-so.' Then the wizard said: 'Sit down here and tell me where he is.' 'I have work to do and cannot stay.' And so he went out of the house. Just as the wizard was opening the letter—the letter had magic in it—the roof of the house fell in and struck him down. The boy saw the house tumbling down: 'And serve you right, you wizard,' said he, and turned back to the palace. Then they had supper and he lay down to sleep.

In the morning as he was washing himself out of the jug, he took off his ring and let it fall into the water. The serving women went to empty the jug in the kitchen and the ring fell out into the sink: a serving maid picked it up. The girl next her said: 'It was I emptied the jug, so the ring is mine.' So they started quarrelling which of them should have it. The princess heard the dispute and ran up and said: 'What is the matter here?' 'We have found this ring here.' The princess looked at it and recognized by the mark on it that it was her own ring, the ring she had given to her betrothed, the boy of whom there was then no sign or sight: scattered he was like dust before the wind. She fell down in a faint. They sprinkled her with water and brought her to, and she asked where the ring had been found. 'In the jug used by the blackamoor.' How were they to know that the blackamoor was the very man who had been lost?

Then at midday, at the table where many great persons had been invited to do honour to the young blackamoor, there was also the official who had been in love with the princess. The blackamoor was asked how he had come to have the ring. He began at once to tell them, exactly as if he had been narrating a story: 'Once upon a time there was a boy who knew his letters well, and opposite him there used to be a princess sitting; because he was a boy of such promise she had a leaning towards him. Then on the day of the wedding there was another man in love with the princess, and this man was jealous. He went to a wizard and a charm was laid upon the boy. This was that when the boy went aside he could not find the door out, only a flight of steps, and by these he came down into the World Below, and the princess was left all by herself. Now if you people here knew who it was who worked this magic on the boy, what would you do to him?' The official was there right in front of him, and when he heard these words his heart began beating, tick tick, like a watch from France. Everyone at the table answered: 'If we knew the man, at once we would have him cut into little pieces for the dogs to devour him.' At this the blackamoor at once poured water into his plate and mixed up with it the ointment which the wizards had given him, and as he anointed himself he seemed to them just as he had been before, white as white, neither taller nor shorter, the man just as they had known him. Then said he: 'It was this official who worked the magic on me.' The king gave his orders and they cut him into little pieces beginning with his feet and then with his hands, that he should suffer all the more torment; they threw the bits to the dogs, and so they cut him all to pieces. The princess threw off her black clothes of mourning and was married to the boy, and his father was invited to the palace, to live there always. So he made the pair a wedding and a very fine wedding too, all with rejoicings and the fairest diversions.

12

The Sun rises in the West

In my *M.G.F.*, No. 29, which I called *The Sun rises in the West*, I was not able to print a text; the four versions were all so broken and fragmentary I could only say that 'a good version might appear any day'. And in fact it was not long before, in 1953, two fresh versions did appear, Nos. 5 and 6 in the list below. The versions are:

1. SMYRNA: the story is given in outline by Politis in his *Laographiká sýmmeikta*, ii. 120.
2. THERA: given in a German translation by Kretschmer in his *Neugriechischen Märchen*, No. 47, p. 202; my text, 12*a*, below, is a translation of this. It is badly told, and to make it intelligible I have had to alter the text slightly in a few places.
3. CHIOS: printed by Pernot in his *Études de linguistique*, iii. 273; again, not a good text.
4. MYTILENE: a translation in *Folklore*, vii. 151.
5. MACEDONIA: Megas has given an outline of the story in *Laographía*, xv (1953), p. 9.
6. SYMI: Text by Miss Irene Moskóvi in her *Tales of my own Country*, *Παραμύθια τῆς πατρίδας μου*, p. 61. This is my 12*b*, below.

In a paper printed in *Laographía*, xv. 147, *The two Bets, a reconstructed Greek Folktale*, I was able from the then accessible versions, Nos. 1 to 5, to piece together the whole story, and now I am helped by No. 6 from Symi. It must have run much as follows:

There was once a boy skilled in playing the flute, and one day a snake heard him and was so much delighted that he gave him a present of money; and this several times. Finally the snake told the boy that when he died he must bury him in his garden, and from the body would spring up a wonderful tree, a tree which, just as the snake, of which it was in a way an embodiment, changed its skin, in the same way would every year change its leaves. We may note that deciduous trees are not as common in the Levant as they are with us. The man could then challenge visitors to say what the tree was called: in one version we are told that it was a snake-cypress. With Greek self-confidence they would make their bets freely, and they would all get the name wrong, and by this kind of bet the man would make a lot of money. So he became very rich.

But one day there came a cunning rascal, generally a Jew, and induced either his wife or his servant to betray the secret; so the man lost his bet and became very poor. In the Symi version, No. 6, this part of the story is not well told; the man's fortune was money given him by the snake, and he lost it, not by betting on what he thought was a certainty but by ordinary card-playing.

In the second part of the story we hear how he got his money back again. He went off to implore the help of the sun, and, just as he had become rich by betting, the sun told him he could regain his wealth by another bet; though bold it should be a certainty. For to help him the sun said that he would on the next day rise not in the east but in the west; on so incredible a happening the man would be able to place any bet he liked and so could regain his money. The Jew came again and in mockery accepted the new bet and so all was well again. In my *Laographía* paper I have suggested that a better title for the story would be *The two Bets*, or perhaps *The Biter bit*.

So far we have a plain and neatly constructed story, but two variants, Nos. 5 and 6, present an interesting addition which we shall see has been grafted on to it from quite a different story. We are told that when the man was on his way to find the sun he met several characters, all of whom were in some sort of trouble and begged him to find out from the sun what they should do to find relief. In the Macedonian version, No. 5, he met an apple-tree whose crop always failed, and a river the waters of which were sucked away into the ground. In the Symi story, No. 6, he met a girl and her sister who could not find husbands, a fig-tree whose figs were always wormy, and two mountains tormented by perpetually clashing one against the other. This incident of the people asking for help belongs properly and regularly to the quite different story of the man who went out in search for his Luck, of which a version from Kos has been printed in *Forty-five Stories*, No. 35, with a long discussion on Luck and Fate as they appear in Greek stories. As we have in both stories a man in search for a remedy for his troubles, it was quite natural to graft this bit of the Luck story into the story of the Two Bets: in the search episode the two were running parallel.

It is not necessary here to set down in detail all the pieces of advice given by the sun, but the third request in No. 6, my 12*b*, below, that of the clashing mountains does deserve a note. They would never be at rest, said the sun, until clashing together they had caught and crushed a man who was passing between them. This may remind us of some of the requests in versions of the Luck story. Thus in a version from Pontos, quoted in *Forty-five Stories*, p. 366, we hear of an old woman who on her trouble went to seek the advice of the mysterious figure called the Sun-Flower, and she was charged to ask his advice by a turbid river. The Sun-Flower said it would never flow with a clear stream until it had drowned a man who was crossing it; nor would a tottering rock ever rest securely on its base until it had crushed a passer-by. In a Cretan story of this type, quoted ibid., p. 366, we hear of an arrow shot in the air, but it could never come to earth until it had pierced and wounded someone. The underlying idea seems to be that nothing can be at its ease until that for which it came into being has been fulfilled, however mischievous that end may be.

It has been suggested to me that the boy charming the snake by the music of his flute is very Indian in style.

NO. 12*a*. THE SUN RISES IN THE WEST[1]

There was once a lazy fellow who spent his time playing the flute: he was so lazy that he lay down on his face when he played it. As he was playing in this way he noticed a snake, and the snake was so much pleased with the music that it brought him a hundred francs as a present. When he brought this money home to his wife, she asked him: 'And where did you steal it?' He answered: 'You just take the money and don't be uneasy.' Then again he went off and played the flute, and once more the snake gave him a hundred francs. When for the third time he went to the same place and played, the snake said: 'I am sick and my end has come. You must dig here and you will find my body. And when you have found me, take me and bury me in your garden.' This the flute-player did, and in the place where he buried the snake there grew up a beautiful tree, which bore (according to his wish) fruit of two kinds, quinces and oranges.

One day there came a sea captain, and from a distance he saw the oranges. He liked them and went to the tavern and

[1] Thera; a translation from the German of Kretschmer's *Neugriechische Märchen*, No. 47, p. 502.

said that never had he seen such oranges. As he was saying this, it chanced that the owner of the tree was in the tavern, and he made a bet that the fruits were quinces. The captain said: 'How can you be so stupid as to make out that they are quinces, when all the time they are oranges? What will you bet me? I will wager my whole ship.' The man wagered him the tree and his wife as well. Next day the tree was clearly loaded with quinces, so the man who owned the tree won the bet and the ship was his.

After this there came a Jew with a basket full of glass ware of various sorts. This man too saw the tree with quinces on it and they were so fine that he liked them very well indeed. So he wagered his basket and all the glass ware in it that they were quinces. The owner wagered the tree and his ship as well that they were oranges. Next morning the tree was bearing oranges and the owner had won the bet, and the basket of glass ware was his.

But this Jew was a cunning fellow and he went off back again to his village. When he had seen to his business there he came back again and looked out for the wife of the man who owned the tree, and he said to her: 'I will let you have all the glass ware I have here with me.' The woman accepted it and wanted to pay him. But he came that way again and said to the woman: 'The money I do not want; it is your help I want.' Then he gave her back the money saying: 'I want you to tell me what is the secret of this tree.' She answered: 'My husband was a lazy fellow and he was one day out playing his flute and a snake came to him. Then he brought the snake here and he buried it in the garden. The tree from its body bears two kinds of fruit, oranges and quinces.' [Then she told him how to make the tree bear what it was wanted to bear.] The Jew then [with this knowledge] went away and looked for the husband and said to him: 'Let us make a bet that your tree is bearing quinces.' The owner of the tree maintained that it was bearing oranges and he wagered the ship and the tree and his wife as well: the Jew wagered a basket of wares. Next morning the tree was bearing quinces, and the Jew took his winnings and left the flute-player in very ill plight.

When the man was thus left all alone he was very much grieved about this business, and he went off to find the sun to help him. And to the sun he said: 'What can I do to amend my state?' The sun answered: 'Go and find the Jew and make a bet with him that I will rise over Akrotiri [a village to the west] although in the due course I rise over Anaphi [an island lying to the east]. But on that day to help you I will rise over Akrotiri.' Then the man sought out the Jew and said to him: 'Let us make a bet that the sun will rise over Akrotiri.' The Jew answered: 'You fool; the sun rises over Anaphi.' Then for that day they made a bet and the Jew wagered all his winnings and the man wagered his life. In the morning they went out to a field to see where the sun would rise. And in fact the sun did rise over Akrotiri and the man who had wagered his life won the bet. When he had thus won back all his substance, he went to his house and killed his wife. Then he lived at peace in his house and to this very day is enjoying his life there.

NO. 12 *b*. THE SUN RISES IN THE WEST[1]

Once upon a time there lived a fisherman with his wife and his son. One morning as the fisherman was getting ready his gear to go fishing, his wife said to him: 'Won't you take our son with you? All day he sits playing in the sun and I can do nothing with him.' 'I will', said the fisherman, and went off with the boy.

Before they got to the sea the boy stopped by a half-ruined tower which was by the path, and cut a reed and made a flute and began playing on it. 'I don't want to go with you, father', said he to the fisherman. 'I'll stop here and play my flute and when you have done fishing come and take me home with you.' The fisherman had a very great weakness for his son and never opposed him, and so the boy went on playing all sorts of tunes on his flute. Some time went by, and suddenly out from a stone in the ruined tower there came a little snake with golden scales; it raised its head and began to dance to the music of the flute. For some time it

[1] Text from Symi, No. 6 in list above on p. 77.

went on dancing, and finally left the boy a gold coin and hid itself again in the wall. The boy picked up the coin; he was surprised by it, for he had never seen anything so bright; as bright as lightning. But his father, when he came back with a few fish, could not believe his eyes. When they were back in the village they went to the best shop there and with the gold piece bought all sorts of fine things. 'God has had pity on us and has worked His wonders,' said the wife when she had heard the story. 'You must go to the same place to-morrow and again play your flute.'

And this is what in fact he did. Every day the boy used to go to the ruined wall and play his flute, and when the snake had done dancing, it used to give him a gold coin.

The years went by and gradually the fisherman's family became rich. They built a fine house and had servants, and when the boy grew up they betrothed him to the most beautiful young lady of family in the village. The marriage soon took place with great rejoicings and festivities. But what with the preparations for the wedding and all the feasting, the boy never had time to go to visit his friend the snake and to play the flute to him. However, as soon as he was quiet again he took his wife and they went to the ruined tower. He sat down with her by the broken wall and began to play on his flute. He played and played but to no purpose: the snake did not show himself. Very much vexed, the boy took a pick-axe and began to break down the old wall. When he had broken it down he found that under the foundation there was an enormous cauldron full of gold coins, and above it there was the snake dead. He wept for the snake as if for his most loved friend and buried it in the garden of his house. With the money, which he conveyed to his house by night so that no one should see him, he bought more fields and became the richest man in the village and in all the neighbourhood. So he and his wife and their children, who had very soon been born, lived a life of great happiness.

But one day, as he was sitting in the tavern with some of his friends, a man who was jealous of him came up to him and persuaded him to play cards. They played all day long and the young man was continually losing, and this wicked fellow gradually won all his money. Finally he won from him all his lands too. The young fisherman was in torment, and hoping to win back what he had lost staked even his house at the game. When he had lost his house, he staked his wife and his children, and in this way the wicked man had them all as his slaves.

Full of despair the young fisherman walked away at random all among the valleys and water-courses, asking himself: 'What can I do now? How can I win back all that I have lost and redeem my wife from slavery and my children too? Oh! to what has my wrongheadedness brought me! Who will help me to get out of this trouble?' He thought and he thought; he struck his head, and at last he said: 'I must go and find the sun. The sun will help me and give me good advice.' But then, how could he find the sun? he did not know where his palace was. He was in despair, and so he went on and began to inquire of everyone whom he met on the way. He walked and he walked all day and all night, and all at once he found himself in front of a little house. By the side of the house he saw an oven hot and ready, and there was a girl sweeping out the oven with her breasts. The young man lost no time, but cut a branch from a tree near by and plunged it into water and quenched the fire in the oven. 'Thank you, my good man,' said the girl, 'for what you have done for me. Sit down and eat something and rest yourself.' 'I can't stop, my girl,' he answered, 'because I have a long way before me. I have to go and find the sun, for I must tell him of my troubles.' 'The sun!' said the girl in astonishment. 'His palace is a long way from here. But as you are on your way there to ask advice for yourself, ask him for me and my sister. What can we do to get married?' 'With great pleasure,' said the young fisherman, and as soon as he had hastily eaten what the girl and her sister had set before him as a guest, he went on again.

After a few hours he found a fig-tree. 'Where are you going, my lad?' said the fig-tree. 'I am going on my way to find the sun. Do you perhaps know where his palace is?' 'I do know,' answered the fig-tree. 'But when you meet him, please beg him to help me, and ask him: what must I do to prevent my figs being all eaten by worms.' 'With great pleasure,' answered the boy, and went along the path which the fig-tree had pointed out to him.

He walked all the night and in the morning he came to two mountains, which were first standing apart, and then closing together again. 'Where are you going this way?' they asked him. 'I am going to find the sun. Let me pass.' 'We will let you pass', said the mountains, 'if you will give us your word that you will ask him about us: what must we do to be free from this opening and closing.' 'I give you my word I will,' said the boy, and the mountains let him pass. He went on till he came to a great plain, and soon he found himself in front of the palace of the sun, which was made all of gold. The mother of the sun, a very fine old woman, was astonished when she saw him and said: 'And how have you come here, my boy? A place to which not even a bird on the wing can come.' The young fisherman told her what had happened to him and said that he had come to ask the advice of the sun. The old woman sighed and said to him sorrowfully: 'To no purpose have you come all this way, my lad. My son is an ogre; and the moment the sun sees you he will devour you.' 'Help me, my dear Mother in Christ,' said he, as he knelt before her. 'Have compassion on my wife and my children who are in slavery to the wicked man.' 'I will do what I can,' said the old woman, and she dealt him a light blow on the cheek. Thus she turned him into a gold vase, and she placed it on the shelf.

After this she began to make ready bread and cooked a dish for her son. She ordered the servant girls instead of the one ovenful of bread which they prepared every day to make two and instead of the two cauldrons of food to make ready four. When in the evening the sun came, he shouted out as he kissed his mother: 'Mother, there is here a savour of man's flesh.' 'And however could there be a man here, my son? Come and eat, for you are hungry and that is why you think there is a savour of man's flesh.' The sun ate the two ovenfuls of bread and the four cauldrons of meat and sat down very well pleased. 'Good for you, my mother. Today you have cooked for me plenty of food, and savoury. I am near bursting.' 'Do you mean that, my son?' said his mother cunningly. 'Suppose you saw a man in front of you now, could you manage to eat him?' 'But how could I? I am full up to the neck,' said the sun. 'But I should like a man to come here and have a talk to him before I go off to sleep.' This emboldened the old woman, and she took the vase down from the shelf and struck it with her hand. Then the boy again took his shape as a man and sat down by the side of the sun and told him all his story. When the sun heard it, he was moved to compassion and said: 'Do not be troubled, my lad; I will help you. To oblige you, one day I will rise in the west and not in the east. Now you must go and make a bet on this with the rascal, and so you will win back again all your wealth and your wife and your children as well.' 'I thank you, my lord sun,' said the young man, 'but just now as I was on the way to you I met two girls and also two mountains, and they begged me to ask what advice you would give them.' Then the sun said: 'The mountains will stay at rest only after they have crushed a man. Therefore when you pass between them you must not tell them this secret but you must start by saying: "I went to the sun and talked to him and he talked to me and I to him and so on", and only when you are a long way off are you to say, "to cease this opening and shutting, it must be that you crush a man." Do not make a fool of yourself and tell them this while you are still near: if you do they will be your death. And with the fig-tree you must do the same. Not until you are a long way off must you shout and say that for the figs not to be all eaten with worms someone must dig deep down at the roots of the tree and throw away the earth and put in new earth. Don't say this when you are near, because the tree is a witch and she will set you to do the digging yourself. To the two girls—and they too are witches—you are to say that they must by force lay hold of some man who is passing by, and one of the two must make him her husband. Then and thus the other one will at once find a husband. But to stop them from laying hold on you by force and making you the husband, as long as you are near them you must say to them as you said to the mountains and to the fig-tree: "I said to him and he said to me and I said to him and so on." Then when you are a long way off you may shout and tell them the secret. Do you understand?' 'I understand, O my lord the sun,' said the young fisherman, and when he had expressed his thanks he set off on his way back to his own country.

He followed all the advice given him and after cunningly escaping from the mountains, from the fig-tree, and from the two girls, he reached his village. Then he made his way to the tavern frequented by the cunning rascal. 'Oh, welcome to you, my lad,' said he in a mocking way. 'Perhaps you would fancy another game of cards with me? But what shall be our stakes, now that you have nothing left?' 'Oh no,' said the young fisherman. 'We won't play cards. We will make a bet, and, if I win, then you will give me back my wealth and my wife and my children. If I lose, then you may take me too to be your slave.' 'And what bet are we to make?' said the rascal with some curiosity? 'Here is the bet,' said the young fisherman. 'I bet you that tomorrow the sun will rise in the west and not in the east. Will you accept this bet?' The rascal laughed mockingly. 'Why, for sure I will accept it, because that way I shall make you my slave. Is it possible that the sun can ever rise in the west? You have for sure gone crazy.' 'That we shall see,' answered the young fisherman.

At dawn next day not only the two who had made the bet but everybody went up on the flat roofs of their houses to see in what quarter the sun would rise. Most of them were sorry for the young fisherman, because they were sure that he would lose. And here they were right: who had ever heard of the sun rising in the west? For all that before very long the wonderful event happened. The sun really did show himself in the west. Everyone in delight embraced and kissed the young fisherman, and the rascal, just as if he had been scalded, ran away from the village as fast as he could, leaving behind him all the wealth and the substance which he had won so dishonourably.

The young fisherman again became a man of great good fortune, and for many years lived with his wife and his children. But never again did he touch a playing-card.

13

The Man who pretended to be dead

THIS Pontic story of a man who, to trick a priest, pretended to be dead, and was then actually killed by the priest is an echo of several stories of men who blasphemously pretended to be dead and were punished by being stricken by death in good earnest. Here are a few examples. In a Greek collection of 'Lives of the Saints', the *Synaxaristís*, set in order by Nikódimos of Mount Athos and published in Zákynthos in 1868, we read, i. 267, under the date 17 November, of St. Gregory the Miracle-worker of Neo-Kaisareia, that in some way he brought about the death of a Jew who had pretended to be dead in order to mock the saint. In the *Golden Legend*[1] we read of a man who shammed dead in order that his friends might collect money for his funeral from the charitable Epiphanius: they found him in actual fact dead. Recently a friend told me of a similar punishment in Russia for some such blasphemous play by a Bolshevik.

NO. 13. THE MAN WHO PRETENDED TO BE DEAD[2]

There was in the course of the years a village which found itself without a priest, and how could the villagers do without a priest? So they said: 'Let us make a man from our village a priest.' So they set apart a man who was one of the best Christians there and they took him off to the bishop. 'Holy Bishop, here are ten pounds for you; make this man a priest.' The bishop made the man a priest and taught him how to say Mass. So the priest began saying Mass. All his lessons from the bishop he had swallowed down just like soup. The service of Mass in the village went on finely.

One day one of the villagers died and the priest was sent for to read the funeral service. The priest was taken aback and in a difficulty. The bishop had quite forgotten to teach

[1] *Legenda aurea*, Graesse's edition, 1846, cap. cxxxviii, p. 616, under the heading St. John Chrysostom; and in Wyzewa's French translation, p. 130.

[2] Text from Pontos; printed in *Pontiakà Phylla*, Year I (1937), Part 11, p. 17.

him the funeral service. So what was he to do? He thought and thought again, and then he said to them: 'Nowadays there is a new custom and the priest stays in the church all alone with the body.' The villagers believed this. So the priest locked the door of the church and began to chant over the dead man just whatever came into his head. Then they carried the body off to burial.

Some days later a villager, who was a clever fellow and a bit of a rogue, said to the other villagers: 'We must do something to find out what it is the priest chants over the dead. I tell you: I must play the dead man, and you can shroud me and set me in the coffin and carry me off to the church. You must lament as loudly as ever you can.' 'Nothing easier', said the villagers. At once they dressed him in a shroud and put him into the coffin, and away with it into the church! One of them went and told the priest. The priest came and sent them all out of the church and then locked the door. Then he took the censer in his hand and rolled up his sleeves and without saying anything at all began to caper about on the coffin. The dead man was near to laughing; but then how could he? The priest would have heard him. As he went on the priest began to go faster: you might have thought someone was running after him. The dead man could stand no more; he burst out laughing and caught the priest by the leg. The priest was so much frightened that he thought the dead man was playing the vampire, and he began hitting him on the head with the censer, and in the end he killed him. Then he opened the door and came out and called to the villagers: 'You sons of dogs! Another time you must let the souls of the dead get properly out of their bodies, and then you can bring them into the church!'

14

The loving Brothers

To this story from Zákynthos on the familiar theme of brotherly love I know of no precise parallel. That the elder of two brothers should be so much the finer, the handsomer, and the stronger of the two is so much against the usual run of these stories, in which the younger brother is always the dominant of the two, that it may be a personal variant of the common theme, turned by some clever story-teller, as one might say, inside out, rather as the story of *The Boy's Dream* in *M.G.F.*, No. 53, appears in No. 7 above, and to my knowledge this once only, as a story of a girl's getting into trouble for a supposedly presumptuous dream of her future triumph over her father.

NO. 14. THE LOVING BROTHERS[1]

There was once a king, and by his first wife he had a boy from whose beauty shone a brightness as of the sun. All the great lords in the palace took thought in the matter, and when the child was christened he was called Born of the Sun. In a little while, however, the queen died, and the king, who could not live alone, married again. This second wife also bore him a son, but never could he attain to the beauty of Born of the Sun, a boy with such hair that when he combed it all the room shone with light! But this second boy was feeble and pale, and because he had been born at midnight they called him Born of the Moon.

When the boys grew big, the stepmother could not endure this; it was poison for her to see her own son such a feeble creature. Every care was taken of him. Doctors, as we say, up in his room; doctors down again; medicines; but no good. So she was very jealous of Born of the Sun, who was as beautiful as a rose; when he combed his hair the whole room was filled with light. And so the queen said to the king that

[1] Text from Zákynthos; printed in *Laographía*, x. 439.

the doctors had declared that, for her son to be well, he must eat his brother's heart; cooked for him. And what was the poor king to do? She entreated him incessantly with tears, and at last the king gave orders for Born of the Sun to be killed. But Born of the Moon had heard what they said: yet how could his mother ever have imagined that he would betray her? Well; he told Born of the Sun about it: 'I must tell you, brother, they said this and that about us,' and so on. 'But for me: to win my health from your blood; never!' Like brothers they embraced and kissed one another. But when Born of the Sun heard what had been said: 'O my brother,' said he, 'for you I would give even my life.'

So the two brothers made up their minds to leave the king's palace. They went on and on, over mountains and through woods, and every now and then Born of the Sun used to take his brother pickaback because he was weak from sickness. When it was night they said they would take a rest, and Born of the Moon said: 'I am thirsty.' 'Stay where you are and I'll see about that,' said Born of the Sun. Tired as he was, the poor fellow went off to find some water, and he brought him a little in his cupped hands, but he found his brother dead of thirst. All night he sat there weeping over him. In the morning he rose up and dug a grave and buried him in it. So he went on and on, and on the way he met a monk: this was Christ. When He saw the boy thus full of sorrow, He said: 'What is the matter, my boy, that you are weeping?' 'Oh,' said he, 'I have lost my brother, and now I am all by myself in the world.' The monk was sorry for him, and even as the boy was speaking he saw his brother standing before him alive. 'Now, my boys,' said the monk, 'come to my cottage, for I have no sons. Come with me and all my living we shall share together.'

The hermit's cottage was in another kingdom, and as they were going into the town there, they heard wailing and lamentations. Then Born of the Sun asked: 'What is the matter here, boys?' 'Oh,' said a man, 'it is an ogre, and he never spares either young man or girl. And now that all of us here are at an end and we have no more blood to give him, he will leave our domains completely exhausted.' The king had sent out a proclamation that whoever could find him a girl or a boy to devote to the ogre, to that man he would give all his royal rights. So then all those who had seen the monk and the two young men ran off to the palace. 'O my king, there is a man here, a man who looks like the sun. Never in all his days has the ogre had such a lad to devour.' 'Bring him here to me at once,' said the king. And for this they brought out the very finest horses from the king's stable. The monk and the boys had sat down to eat, when they heard the trampling of feet. 'Oh and alas,' said the monk, 'now we are lost.' He opened a little door which was there in the cottage and led the boys down under the earth. The men, who were carrying out the king's orders, broke open the door of the cottage. 'Give me the boy, old man.' The monk said: 'He is not here; search for him yourselves.' The men did not believe this, and began to take the stick to him, and with salt too. From down below Born of the Sun heard the cries. 'I must go up there,' said he. 'For charity's sake I cannot endure that they should beat my kind elder like that.' He rushed out upon them: 'Here I am,' said he. 'What more do you want?' 'We must take you off to the king.' Said he: 'We will go.'

When the princess saw the beauty of Born of the Sun, at once she loved him. 'O my father,' said she, 'this man is from God and now he is in your hands. Do not send him off to the ogre.' The king could not do as she wanted. How could he, when the ogre was making such an outcry that the whole town was shaking with fear? 'Fresh blood; I can smell it. Bring me it or I shall murder you,' shouted the ogre again and again. But could the princess let Born of the Sun leave her side? No; she gazed at him and could never have enough and would have all done as she wished. Then the king grew angry and commanded that both of them should be sent off to the ogre.

All along the way they were weeping, each of them so sorry for the other. This the ogre heard and had compassion on them: a miracle worked by Christ because of the way Born of the Sun had dealt with his brother. The ogre qucstioned them and heard their story, and then he said: 'Go off and good luck be with you!' So with great joy they went off to the palace. Only one thing for the king to do! When he saw them back again, he found a priest and a best man and crowned the pair in marriage.

But Born of the Moon had scarcely seen the bride than he fell in love with her. He began to weep; to eat nothing; never to say a word. Whatever they could do to make him speak, he would say nothing, but from day to day he grew thin and wasted like a wax candle. Well, not to make a long story of it, the time came when they would give him the last sacrament. 'O my father,' said he to the priest, 'and how can I live, when this lady is before me all day and I cannot touch her because she is my brother's wife?' Born of the Sun was behind the door and heard this talking. He had been sure that his brother would say this to the priest, and so of set purpose he was on watch. 'O my little brother,' said he, 'haven't you seen? Don't you know me? Why should it have been so hard for you to say this to me? Better that my wife should be your own very wife than that I should lose my brother.' Then Born of the Moon began to get better, and they lived happily, and so may we in even greater happiness.

15

The two Kings

IN this story from Rhodes, which I have called *The two Kings*, the familiar theme of the blessing or curse of a father serves as the introduction to the story, the central theme of which is a study of the characters of the two brothers: rather like No. 24 below, *The two Pauls*. Here the elder of the two is a man so naturally base that he wants above all things to inherit his father's wealth, and no considerations of piety or desire for a blessing rather than a curse hold him back; the younger is a man of virtue, who knows that his father's blessing is of more importance than any material advantage. When we ask why the elder brother came to ruin, we are given only his own way of presenting the fact, the pious opinion that it was by God's will. To the general line of the story details are irrelevant; we are left to suppose that it was in some characteristic way his own fault.

I know of no parallel to this story, the style of which approaches very closely to such novels as Nos. 23 and 24 below. The manner of narration is a little verbose and I have felt compelled in a very few places to do a little pruning of verbal repetitions. There are a few folktale commonplaces: the hero's successful management of the tavern; the hospitable old woman; and the keeping of the fallen queen in the henhouse. The reason why the sailors are reluctant to help the blinded hero would be more obvious in a Greek village than to us: it is the idea that any over-generous kindness to an outcast person who has no special claim to assistance is supposed to be rather unlucky; to have an element of danger; to be a kind of tempting of Providence. Here compare No. 16 below, against the adoption of children.

In many stories we read of eyes being destroyed and then restored, and generally as blue instead of black, in which case the change does not merely hinder recognition but is regarded as unpleasant. Blue is in fact not a good colour for eyes; all right for the wicked Turkish lady but not for a good king. Blue eyes, says Burton in his *Arabian Nights*, Library edition, iii. 311, have a bad name in Arabia and in eastern countries. In Crete they are taken as a sign that a man has the evil eye. The fact seems to be that in all these countries blue eyes are so unusual as to be disagreeable.

NO. 15. THE TWO KINGS[1]

Red thread twisted well,
Neatly wound upon the reel;
Set the reel a-turning, do,
And I'll tell a tale to you,
To all this noble company;
And may the time pass pleasantly.

And this is the beginning of the story; a good evening to you. Stand aside, and I will tell it to you from the beginning.

In that time and in those years there was a king, and when that king was at point to die, he called for his two sons and divided his substance between them. One half of what he had to leave was his blessing: that and nothing more. The other half was his curse and with it went all his goods. When he had made this division of his substance, the elder son was very well content that his brother should have the blessing, and he have his father's curse, for with it went the property.

When the father died the younger son went away, and came to a city which belonged to another king. Then he bethought him where he should lodge, and as he was thinking about this, he came upon an old man who kept a tavern. 'My old man, will you not let me stay with you for a little while that I too may have a little bread to eat?' The old man of the tavern said: 'I can't earn enough to eat, and how can I do anything for you?' 'Never mind about that, my old man: when I am with you, God will help us.' So the man accepted him, and the prince came to his shop. At once he took charge of the tavern; he whitewashed it right and left, and polished up all the coffee pots. Then the couple of customers the old man had came and were very well pleased with the boy's service. Afterwards many others came to the shop and were very well pleased, and so the vizier heard of it; he too came and was delighted. The boy knew well that it was the vizier and bowed to him in a suitable manner, and the vizier when he went away brought out a handsome present and laid about twenty gold pieces on the tray. Then he went off to

[1] Text from Rhodes; printed in *Laographia*, v. 626.

the king and told him that there was a fine young chap in the old man's tavern. The king therefore disguised himself and went to the old man. The boy recognized that it was the king and bowed before him in a fitting manner. The king too was very well pleased, and when he went away he left in the tray about fifty gold coins as a present. The king liked the boy and thought of taking him as a son-in-law, marrying him to his daughter. He sent for the boy to the palace and said to him: 'My boy, take these account books rendered by my twelve counsellors and reckon them up.' When the boy had looked into the books he found many things in them put down wrong; at once the king banished all the twelve, and he married the boy to his daughter. After the wedding the young prince issued a decree to the men in the city: 'Whoever has a hundred to pay, let him pay twenty; and whoever has twenty to pay, let him pay five.'

When his father-in-law was dead, the new king remembered his brother, and so he told four soldiers to go to his brother's city to see how he was. So they went and looked for the king but they could not find him. The people told the soldiers that he was 'up on that mountain over there'. So the soldiers went to the mountain and there they found him, naked and miserable, going this way and that crying for his children. The soldiers questioned him, and he said: 'My luck has brought me here to keep the swine.' The soldiers said: 'Your brother the king has sent us to bring you to him.' When he heard this he was very happy and said: 'Let us go.' So they loaded up his filthy old tent and all of them went to the city. When the younger brother saw his condition he ordered the bathman to take him to the bath, him and his wife and his children. Then he ordered his servant to bring royal robes for his brother and his wife and special clothes for his two children. Further he commanded his servants: 'Food you must serve first to my brother and to us afterwards.' When all this had been done the two brothers talked, and told what had happened to each of them. The younger brother asked the elder how it was that his kingdom had come to ruin. 'This was the will of God,' answered the elder.

Let us now consider the men of the city. They were very well pleased with their king, and in such prosperity that every day they feasted joyfully. Then the wife of the elder brother conceived a wicked idea and said to her husband: 'I can never be happy unless you are made king here.' Her husband said: 'My wife, how can I be fit to be king, I who have kept the swine?' His wife persisted and said: 'This is the way: you must kill your brother.' Her husband said: 'How can I kill my brother? Why, I don't know how.' The woman said: 'I will show you how. Tomorrow you shall make out that you are sick and your brother will ask you what is the matter. And when he asks you, then you must say you are not well. And if he says to you, "What do you want?" you must say, "Is it possible for us to go out for a little walk?" Then if he says, "Where?" you must say, "To the castle", and you must go to the part of the castle over the sea. Then you must stoop down and say to him: "Is that a ship down below there?" And when he comes and stoops down to see if there is a ship, then you must push him over.'

So when it was morning the man pretended to be ill. When his younger brother went to see him, he found him very sad, and asked him: 'What is the matter, brother?' He said: 'When I was away I used to live out in the woods, and in here I feel unwell; if it is possible I should like to go out and have a pleasant walk.' 'And where shall we go, my brother?' 'Let us go to the castle.' Then the younger brother told two of his faithful guards to bring two horses and make ready for their outing. The guards brought the horses and the two brothers mounted and went off. And when they arrived at the castle they told the guards to hold the horses and wait for them. So the brothers went up on the castle, to the part over the sea. Then the elder said to his brother: 'Come here and look at a big ship down there below.' So in all innocence the younger brother went to look, and the elder pushed him over into the sea. With the violence of his fall his eyes were blinded. Then feeling his way bit by bit, he found a big rock and sat down upon it.

There let us now leave him and follow the elder brother. He went to the guards and said: 'Let us start off.' The guards said: 'Where is our king?' 'Your king?' said he. 'I am your king. My brother has fallen over the cliff. No more talking.'

So they went up to the town and he let people see him sitting on his brother's throne, and ordered the guards to strip his younger brother's wife of her robes and to put her into the henhouse; there she could live among the fowls.

Now let us pass to the people of the city. From them the king demanded such heavy taxes that they had no rest, day or night. Among themselves they said: 'And what can have happened to our good king?' The people and all their families went into mourning for him.

Now let us leave them chafing under the rule of their new king, and turn to the other brother, now blinded, groaning and lamenting. A fishing boat, whose luck was very much out, was passing that way and the captain heard the man's outcries and came close to him. The sailors said to the captain: 'Have we not enough trouble ourselves? Must we now go helping someone else?' Now when the blinded man heard the sailors talking, he took courage and shouted out: 'To the rescue, my men! Christians are you? Turks? Jews?' When the captain heard him—he was a Turk but a man with a good heart—he said to his sailors: 'Bring the blind man into the ship.' The sailors began grumbling to the captain, saying: 'Is not our own ill luck enough, casting our nets again and again and always for nothing, that we should take upon ourselves any more trouble?' Then said the captain: 'Oh, just a cup of coffee, please, for the poor blind man!' Next time they cast their net there was nothing in it at all, not even a sprat. Then the sailors began saying to the captain: 'Other times when we cast the net, we used anyhow to catch something; now nothing at all.' The blinded man heard this and said privily to the captain: 'O my captain, man of gold, I beg you to make a cast in the name of the blind man.' Then they cast the net and began to draw it up again, but they could not. The sailors said to the captain: 'Other times anyhow we pulled up the net all safe; this time it must be all tangled: we will kill that blind man.' When the captain heard this he said: 'No, my lads. I beg you not to lay a hand on the blind man. Get a good grip and just draw up the net gently.' Then they took a good grip and pulled up the net; it was loaded and heavy, and when it was half up they saw that it was full of fish. They went on pulling it up with even greater care. Then said the captain to the sailors: 'What do you say now about the blind man? Has he brought you any harm? It is God has sent him to us. Now load the ship and take her to the town; sell the fish and bring more boats here that we may take off the rest of the fish.' When the boats came the sailors loaded them with the fish and sold them in the town, and there were a hundred gold pieces to share out. Then the captain took the blinded man to his house and said to his Turkish wife: 'First to the blind man you must serve food; to us afterwards.' And he went on to say: 'Give all good care to the blind man.'

Some time after this the sailors and the captain had a demand for fish; in a village in the country where they were with their boat there happened to be a festival. The captain had taken his wife with him that she might look after the blinded man. So they cast the net and without leaving it down at all they drew it up again, and it had in it five loads of fish. The men said among themselves: 'Let us take with us two or three loads of fish and take the blind man as well that in accordance with his religion he may go to the feast.' They made ready and said to the blind man: 'As your religion bids us, let us go up to the festival.' The blind man was not much pleased at this, for he said: 'I am blind; I can't see the sports; I shouldn't know how to dance; what would there be for me to do at the festival?' To humour the blind man the captain said to his wife: 'You stay here in the boat and amuse him.' When the captain had gone off, the devil entered into the woman to make her vex and plague the blinded man. He said to her: 'I will not dishonour the bread I have from the captain.' The woman saw that the blinded man would not do this wickedness, and she resolved to denounce him to the captain. When the captain and the sailors were on their way back, she on the prow of the ship had torn her clothes and was crying aloud: 'Oh, save me!' When the captain and the sailors saw this, they ran to the rescue of the lady and cried out that they would kill the blind man. The blinded man heard them and said to the captain: 'O my captain, you who are a man of good heart, have patience, and let me say something to you; then do with me as you wish.' The captain said to the sailors: 'Have patience and let the blind man speak. Speak then, you blind man.' The blind man said to the captain: 'Since you have had me in your ship I have fared well, because, for all that you are a Turk, you are a man of good heart. This is on my honour the truth, and as a sign may your ship split into two halves, and I be in one half and the lady in the other, and to make you believe me, may the eyes of your wife come out of her head and come into mine: from the very hour you went away she has been a plague to me.' When the blinded man had done speaking, oh, what a marvel! the boat did split in two, and there was he in one half and the Turkish lady in the other; out came the eyes of the woman and went into his head; the only thing was that the eyes now in his head were blue. Then said the blinded man to the captain and the sailors: 'Do you now believe me? And if you don't believe me, I will go off in the one half of the ship and the lady in the other.' Then they shouted out: 'It is all true, O blind man, and we do believe you: so now come off out of the ship.' And then, when the blinded man had left his half of the ship, the two halves came together again into one. Then said the captain to the blinded man: 'You are indeed a man of truth,' and he bowed low before him. 'Now, my captain, I beg you to grant me my freedom.' 'No,' said the captain, 'I must have you with me.' And the blinded man said: 'Oh no, my captain; our fellowship was to be up to this moment only.'

Let us now leave the blinded man on his way to his city and look at the captain and his sailors. They said to the captain's wife: 'And why did you tempt and trouble the blind man?' The woman said: 'Indeed, my master, I was to blame. I am in your hands and do to me as you please.'

Let us now leave them to their perilous life at sea, and look at the king who had gone off to his city. He saw the people's houses hung with black and thought it over: 'There is something going on here. I must find some old woman with a cottage in an out-of-the-way place and lodge there.' Walking on he did find an old woman in a little house. He said to her: 'Will you take me in as your guest?' The old woman said: 'I am willing, but I have neither bedding nor food.' 'Never mind about that, my old woman.' So the king went into the house and gave the old woman one or two gold pieces and ordered her to bring to the house everything necessary. Then she went all round the market making her purchases. Lighting the lamp, she looked at his face. Then she said in her heart: 'He is very like our good king but for one thing: his eyes are changed; this man's are blue and the king's were dark.' Then the old woman questioned the king: 'We used to have here a good king and you are very like him; tell me, won't you?' He said: 'I am indeed the man.' They sat down at the table and ate; the old woman had cooked plenty of food. He gave her one or two glasses of wine, and she became a little tipsy. Then said he: 'You know what has become of the queen, don't you?' 'Yes, I know; we are keeping her very closely shut up; she lives with the fowls.' 'Can't you speak a word to her and let her know that I am here in your house?' The old woman, tipsy as she was, understood the danger of death from the elder brother: he was keeping the queen shut up there and no one ever speaking to her. How could she go there? But the old woman took courage and by the light of the moon, passing from one dark shadow to another, she came to the palace. Then she went to the henhouse outside, where the fowls were kept. The old woman said to the princess: 'Will you not come forward, my princess? I have something good to tell you.' She answered: 'What spirit of the air are you that you come here to torment me?' And saying this the princess made a terrible outcry. The old woman ran away in terror; before she reached her house her soul all but left her. The king saw her terror and asked her: 'Why are you so much frightened, my old woman?' 'There was a terrible outcry and they ran after me and in fear I ran off.' Then said the king: 'Take this ring and show it to her and then come back.' When the old woman came again to the queen in the henhouse, she showed her her husband's ring. When the queen saw the ring, she broke open the door; at the noise the old woman started to run off quickly to her house. The queen caught her up and they both entered the house together. The queen said to the old woman: 'Where did you find my husband's ring?' The old woman said: 'He gave it to me.' 'And where?' 'Here in my house. Indeed your husband is here.' 'O my God, and is this a dream or is it the truth?' Then said the king to the queen: 'It is the truth.' The queen fainted. The king lost no time but took her in his arms and recovered her. Then they spoke of many things and of the state of the men of the city and of the realm. Then the king had good plenty of food made ready and they sat down and ate until it was dawn, and time for the queen to go off to where she lived and no one notice her. The queen knew the place, and next evening she went there again and she and the king agreed what they should do, and what would be the best occasion for him to ascend the throne: it was to be when the elder brother had gone to church.

So they set some men to tell them when the elder brother went off to church, and when he was told it was the time, the king went to the palace. But because his eyes were changed, the guard did not recognize him and said: 'What do you want here?' 'I am your king; do you not know me?' The guards looking at him somehow saw signs that he was the king and they were so much delighted that they lowered their weapons and cried out: 'Oh, our good king, oh, our good king!' Said the king: 'Bring the queen up here.' When they had brought her and the church service was over, the king, the elder brother, came to the palace: he saw there was a great disturbance and asked everywhere what had happened.

Let us now leave him asking what was going on, and consider his younger brother, the good king. He said to his guards: 'Arrest my brother in the palace and his wife and his children.' After the arrest people gathered together to see what was happening. The guards proclaimed to the crowd: 'Our good king has come back to us.' Then the people rejoicing at the coming of the good king and moreover sorely chafing at their heavy taxes, said to the guards: 'Is all this true or is it false?' The guards said to the good king: 'The people are calling for you; they want to express their joy and their thankfulness.' The king went out on his balcony, but the people said: 'Our king, the good one, had black eyes; this man is like him to look at but his eyes are blue.' 'You are right in this, my sons. This was a trick of my brother's. He was keeping the swine and I brought him to royal estate and it was through him my eyes were changed.' Then the king began to tell the people the tale from the beginning. Then the elder brother said: 'I have sinned against my younger brother.' Then the younger brother ordered him to be set to live in another palace and assigned him a good living. Then he granted the men of the city all their freedom and he himself lived even better.

But I was not there and you are not to believe the story.

16

Do neither Kindness nor yet Unkindness

THIS story from the Greeks of the neighbourhood of Smyrna is not well told, and I have found it necessary to add a few words, always put in brackets, to help out the sense: even so, the curse of the tree grown in the brother's ear is not very plain, and the way he is delivered by his sister and her child even less so. It may be suspected that the story has lost clearness by being told by someone who did not quite understand it. That a snake inside a person can be induced to crawl out by putting hot milk, as a bait, close to the sufferer's mouth, is well known, though I doubt if the narrator of the story was very clear about it.

The title of the story suggests at first sight that the moral is the usual one in Greece: do not go to excess in anything, even in doing good, but perhaps the idea here is even more that adopted children are dangerous: they are as perverse and wicked as a man's own children are by nature grateful and respectful to their parents. Of this many examples could be quoted. An example from Kos is in the story *The high King*, No. 26 in *Forty-five Stories*. In it we read that the only person who would volunteer to act as executioner is the very man who, as a child, had been brought up by the victim's charity. See also note on No. 15, above.

NO. 16. DO NEITHER KINDNESS NOR YET UNKINDNESS[1]

There was once a father, and he had two children. He said to them: 'My children, in this world neither kindness should be done nor yet unkindness.' Then came a time when the father died, and the mother too. They had had vineyards, fields, gardens: all manner of good things. One day the girl said to the boy—the boy was the younger—that they must go to their vineyards and their fields to look after their

[1] Text from Vourlá near Smyrna, printed in *Mikrasiatiká Khroniká*, iv. 270, No. 14.

gardeners. So they sent an order for horses for them to ride and go to their gardens.

As they were on the way, they heard in a bush a sound of crying: it was the crying of a child. 'My brother,' said the girl, 'here in the bush is a child crying.' 'My sister, what did our father say to us? Neither kindness must you do, nor yet unkindness.' 'I must go, my brother, and see what it is there crying. I can't go on and leave it.' So she went, and there she saw a child crying: it lay there naked. She cut her shift in two and covered the child. 'O my sister, and what did our father say? That we should do neither kindness nor unkindness.'

So they took the child home and found a nurse for it, and brought up the child—it was a girl. The child grew up and so did the boy, and the two of them came to an age to be married. One day the sister said to her brother: 'My brother, I have something to say to you: will you do what I want?' 'Nay, sister; not one request only; two if you like.' 'We now, my brother, are three of us, all of a family. Your share shall be as my share, and my share shall be as the share of our adopted daughter. And if you are willing, of her who is half mine I will give you my half, and you shall take our adopted daughter as your wife.' 'Well, my sister, let it be so. We will ask the priest, and if this be lawful, then I will marry her.' They inquired and it proved to be lawful, and this was the start of the wedding.

A year passed; all went well. Two years passed and all was well. Then in the tenth year the bride grew jealous of her husband, saying that he loved his sister too well. So she set herself to give her sister snakes to eat; she ordered their dairyman to bring three snakes' eggs and to give them to her sister-in-law. In her body the snakes grew big and the girl was very ill indeed. One day at table the brother was crying about his sister's illness. His wife asked him: 'Why are you crying?' 'I am crying about my sister, because of the state I see her in, and when she dies I shall be digging my own grave and be buried there, and yet all alive.' 'What? A brother crying for his sister? If she is sick, it is her own fault.' 'And what is the reason of her sickness?' 'Your sister is with child.' 'And who is the man by whom my sister is with child?'

'I don't know who the man is. But come; see, she is asleep; you lay your hand on her and you will feel the child stirring.' He went and laid his hand on her, and the snake inside her stirred. Then very early in the morning he sent for three butchers and said to them: 'I want you to take my sister away and kill her, and this little flask you must fill with her blood, and bring me also her little finger as a token.'

As they were all going out of the door, behold, there was a lamb with them. They drove it off this way and that way too, but the lamb would not go away; it went off with them. When they had passed right away beyond their vineyards and beyond their fields, the girl said: 'But you are not taking me to our vineyards and fields; where then are you taking me?' 'We are taking you off to kill you.' 'And why will you kill me?' 'Your brother told us to do so. We are to fill this little flask with your blood and to cut off your little finger as a token and bring them to him.' 'Won't it do if you kill this lamb and fill the flask with its blood? You may cut off my finger and take it to him as a token, and you can leave me here, and let the wild beasts devour me.' So they killed the lamb and filled the flask with its blood. Then they roasted it and ate it and left the girl some of it to eat. Then they cut off her finger and went off. The girl remained in that place for four years; with nothing to eat; nothing at all. As the years went on she would be crying out: 'O God, my God, let me see even a bit of cheese, even though I die for it.' God saw into her heart and had pity on her. One day she said: 'Now I must go and find some shepherd and ask him for a slice of cheese, even though I must die for it.'

Her luck brought her to a shepherd; he was the man who used to bring eggs to the milkman. As she was on her way to the sheepfold, the dogs fell upon her and were like to devour her. The shepherd ran up to protect her and to bring her past the dogs: he saw that she was the lady to whom he used to bring eggs. He cried out to his mother: 'Mother, mother; come here quick,' said he. 'What do you want, my son?' said the shepherd woman. 'Run, mother, and milk the sheep and fetch our rope, the long one, and tie it in a noose to the plane-tree; then heat the milk and I will tell you.' So the woman went to milk the sheep and then heated the milk. He himself went there with the girl quite quietly. 'Have you heated the milk, mother?' 'I have, my son.' Then the shepherd turned to the strange girl and said to her: 'Now I am going to do something to you and you must not be frightened; it is for your good.' He took her and tied her [head downwards] to the tree. 'Mother, cover up the milk carefully and bring it here to me.' 'Take a deep breath,' said he to the strange girl. She took a breath and [out of her mouth] there fell from inside her a snake [attracted by the savour of the milk]. It was a snake *so* big; huge. Then he let her down for a rest, and then he boiled up the milk again and once more hanged her up. In the same way another snake fell from inside her. 'Heat up the milk again, mother.' She heated the milk and he hanged her up again. 'Take a deep breath.' She took a breath and the third snake fell from her mouth. 'Run, mother, and bring the cauldron of food and don't keep any of it back; no, not even for me.' The girl sat down and ate; then they led her gently into the sheepfold. The shepherd woman felt such sorrowful love for her that she would by no means suffer her to leave them. As for making her work, not even would she allow the girl to take the water jar in her hand.

One day she said to her: 'My daughter, I have something to say to you. Will you consent to hear what I have to say?' 'O my mother, not only what you want to say will I hear, but if you tell me to go and throw myself into the well, I will do it, after all that I have seen you do for me.' 'Will you take my son for your husband?' 'I would take not your son only but even your very dog.' So the wedding began.

Then they had a child [a daughter], and the mother fell to saying: 'In my brother's ear may a plane-tree rooted be; and unless I go to him, may he from it ne'er be free.' And in her brother's ear a plane-tree did take root. All the doctors in the world went to him. They cut off one twig and straight two more grew up: two they cut and four grew up. No doctor could find a way to save him.

Then one day the girl said to her daughter: 'We will go to your uncle and you shall tell me to give you a sweet and to tell you the word by which the tree will be uprooted.' And so they went. The girl gave her daughter the sweet and the child said: 'One word from me and one twig has gone.' Crack! a twig broke from the tree. Then the child had another sweet, and said: 'Another word from me and another twig gone.' And again the twig broke and the root of the tree only was left. Then the sister began her story from the beginning: 'O my brother, you are my brother and would have had me killed. But the butchers did not kill me; they killed the lamb. And I cursed you and in your ear a plane-tree was rooted. It was no man set life within my body, but your wife filled me with snakes. Then my husband who is our shepherd saved me. And see, here is the finger they cut off. One word from me and the root shall uprooted be.'

Then they took a bag of walnuts and a stallion, and on the horse they tied the bride; for every nut there was to be a piece torn from her body. The brother and sister lived and grew old together.

17

The jealous Sisters

THIS Pontic story has all through a comic tone, and is, I think, to be taken as a parody of the numerous stories of which the theme is a beautiful younger sister and her two jealous elders. That two old women, one of seventy and the other about sixty, should be jealous of the charms of a junior of fifty, and she with no good looks at all left to her, is sufficiently ludicrous, and the rest of the story is to match. The finger sucked white derides the kind of evidence on which a lover believes in the beauty of a hidden girl. The coffer in which the old woman is conveyed is a parody of a bride's marriage procession, and all the more suitable as the bride is already half dead. The old woman pitched out of the window by the infuriated king is comic, and that she should land in a tree reminds us of the beautiful girl who so often in these stories is seen up in a tree and refusing to come down. The very idea of pretending that an old woman is beautiful is in itself intentionally absurd. There are a few other examples of a story-teller making fun of his own art. Thus it is a commonplace that the hero appeases the fury of an ogress by appealing to her as his mother: for which see No. 10, above, and this is parodied in one story by the hero who makes the same pretence about an ogre.[1]

NO. 17. THE JEALOUS SISTERS[2]

There were once three girls who were sisters, and these three were left on the shelf. The eldest of the three was seventy and the youngest was fifty. The unfortunate youngest one was kept always locked up in the big room behind the lattice, and they never let her go abroad and they never opened the window. Their noses ran rheumy with spitefulness and their tongues were of poison. Sometimes too they would leave her starving, and then what could the poor creature do to cheat

[1] An ogre made to believe he is the hero's father is in *M.G.F.*, p. 107.

[2] Text from Pontos; printed in *Pontiaká Phylla*, iii (1938), Part 26, p. 76.

her hunger? She used to suck at her little finger, and from all this sucking her finger became white; it was like milk.

One day she passed her little finger out through the lattice and the king passed by and looked at the window: he saw the white finger and halted and said: 'Such a white finger she has! How great must her beauty be!' And he told his people to put a mark on the door. Next day very early he sent his vizier to the girl's house. The vizier knocked at the door and the eldest sister opened it to him. 'The king has sent me to ask for your daughter: he wants to make her his queen.' 'May the king be well and may his years be many! But tell him that I have no daughter.' 'What do you mean, you have no daughter? The king saw her finger sticking out through the lattice.' Then the woman thought a little and had a pleasant idea; she said to herself: 'Now I will let him see her.' So she said to the vizier: 'Very well, I will let him have her. But she is a girl who has never looked upon the sun ever since she was born, and I am afraid that if the sun sees her suddenly something may happen to her. Let the king send me a coffer and we will put her into it and so she can be taken to the palace.'

The king gave orders and a great coffer all of gold was made, and she was put into it, and the king's men came to take her away to the palace. The eldest sister said to the vizier: 'In the night do not let the king light the lamp or something may happen to my daughter.' So they came to the palace and brought the bride out of the coffer and made her lie down on the bed to have a rest. Evening came on, and in the big room all was as dark as pitch. The king came in to take pleasure in his bride, and he grasped her hand: 'Oh, oh, oh!' she cried. Then he stooped down to kiss her. 'Oh!' she cried again. The man was angry and he lit the lamp to see what was the matter with his bride. Then at once what did he see? What was lying in the bed? It was an old woman. The king became like a wild beast; he seized hold of her, took her up, and pitched her out into the garden. The poor bride was caught in the branches of a tree, and there she was, hanging up in the air.

Inside the king's garden there was a pavilion, and every evening a witch and her three daughters used to come and sit there. This witch was one who never laughed, and this was a great sorrow to her daughters, and they thought what they could do to make her take a little pleasure in something. Somehow the witch saw the old woman hanging there in the branches and swaying in the wind: the moon was shining. At this the witch began laughing. Her daughters were so delighted they jumped for joy. 'How did it happen, mother, how did it happen, and you are laughing?' they asked her. 'And how can I not laugh? Just look and see what has happened to the king. His bride has turned out to be an old woman.' The girls ran and brought the bride down to the ground. 'And how did you get up in the tree?' they asked her. 'The king married me, and when he saw I was an old woman and a thousand times hideous, he pitched me out of the window.' 'As for us, our mother has not laughed for all these so many years and now you have made her laugh. We are grateful to you.' The eldest sister said: 'I will give you my beauty.' The second said: 'I will give you my shapely figure.' The third one said: 'I will give you my lovely hair.' Thus they did, and the old woman became five times fair and there she stayed underneath the tree.

In the morning the king opened the window and he saw a girl, a thousand times fair, sitting below the tree. He went down to see her. 'Who are you?' he asked her. 'I am the bride whom you picked up and threw out of the window.' The king rubbed his eyes and could not believe it. However, he took her into the palace and gave orders for the wedding to be prepared. 'Let us invite my sisters to the wedding,' said the bride to the king; and they were invited. So they came and saw their sister a thousand times fair: they were ready to burst, but yet there was nothing they could say. The wedding feast lasted forty days and forty nights. After the wedding the eldest sister went to the bride and questioned her. 'My dear, how is it that you have become beautiful, even as the sun?' The bride knew that she would see from her sisters many more evil tricks, and bethought her what she could do to escape. 'I will tell you, but you must not tell anyone. The king saw that I was ugly and he gave me money and said to me: "Go away out of the town and find the witch who is in a cave at the foot of the mountain and she will tell you." So I went to the witch and she sent me to an old man in the valley in the forest; I gave him the money and he took off my skin and made me as you now see me.' 'Give me too some money that I may go to him,' said the eldest sister.

So she gave her a pot of money and the woman went to an old man there in the wood and asked him: 'Is it you who made the old woman beautiful? I will give you this money, and make me as she is.' The old man saw the money shining in his eyes; he just killed her and took the money. Days passed and the old woman did not come back. The second sister was much distressed. She questioned the queen, who told her what had happened. Then this second sister also asked for a pot of money, and went off to find the old man. She went on and went on to the end of the wood and looked there and saw the old man. 'Old man, are you he who made the old woman beautiful? Let me give you this money and make me, too, beautiful.' When the old man saw the money it shone bright in his eyes; he killed the old woman and snatched the money.

Thus the queen lived happily and was delivered from her sisters—a pair of snakes.

18

The fated Marriage

In the innocence of the girl this Cretan story has a certain resemblance to No. 45 in *M.G.F.*, *The three Measures of Salt*, in which the girl in an honest way deceives her foolish husband three times, the prophecy being that she will pound on her husband's head three measures of salt, and he be none the wiser.

Several points in the story may be noted. The fates who give the child in accordance with what they themselves happen at the moment to have of wealth or poverty, appear again in No. 35 of *Forty-five Stories*, *A Man and his Luck*; see especially pp. 361 and 364. The episode of a woman recognized by the lullaby which she is singing to her baby appears in *M.G.F.*, No. 14, *The Girl with two Husbands*, and again in the same story in *Forty-five Stories*, No. 36, p. 381.

NO. 18. THE FATED MARRIAGE[1]

What is written by Fate and by Christ, that no axe can do away.

Once upon a time there was a woman, and she longed however it might be to have a child; every day her husband and she used to pray to God to send them a child, and they would make great offerings to the monasteries. They were indeed very rich people and could make very great offerings.

This then was their vow: should they have a child, they would take him to be baptized in a certain monastery which lay out in the country; there too he should be born. Suddenly the woman became with child. Then came the hour of hours when the child should be born; they started on their way to the monastery. When they were still far off, night fell and the woman could go no farther. 'Have patience, and we can go over there yonder where I see a light, and the people will take us in.' Well or ill, they arrived and knocked at the door: out came an old woman. 'Give us a lodging, will you; so may

[1] Text from Crete; printed in *Myson*, vii. 151.

you have good luck. My wife is in this condition and we are benighted.' 'Be so good as to come in.' Inside the house there were other old women sitting, and there were lamps; some burning, some quenched; some half and some fully quenched.

They ate and drank and went to sleep. But the husband could not sleep: all the time he heard rappings. 'I say, what can there be going on in here?' Now and again someone came and knocked, saying: 'Such and such a poor woman has had a daughter; what do you grant her?' The answer was: 'What I have in my hands shall be hers.' The woman who said this was holding a skein of gold thread and winding it. Then in a little while again: rap rap at the door. 'Who is it?' 'A princess has been born; what do you grant her?' The answer was: 'What I have now in my hands shall be hers.' But at that moment the woman was doing no more than just stir the ashes. This went on all through the night.

Then the man heard a voice: 'And this unlucky fellow here taking his wife where she may have her baby?' 'She will die, but the child will live, and live to wear out twelve shifts in no honest wedlock.' A sweat came upon the man. In the morning he and his wife rose up to go away. The man questioned an old woman: 'But what are the people in this house?' She said: 'We are the Fates of men. The lamps burning well are men in good health; those quenched are the dead; and when they are half quenched, these are the lamps of men dying.'

So the two of them went to the monastery, and there the wife bore her baby and then died. 'One of the two things has truly come to pass,' said the man: 'But the other I will never suffer to happen.' He took the baby and a woman to look after her, and then in a place outside the city he built a sheer tower, and locked them up inside it. The baby grew up to be a beautiful girl, and she knew no other people but only the woman and her father. But near by that place the king built a tower, and one day from her window the girl saw the king's son. 'Oh, nurse; a wild monster!' 'No, my child, no monster, but the prince, and he is a human being, and a fine one; just like us.' The girl fell in love with him and the prince with her, and one day she let a rope down to him and brought him up into the tower. This affair went on for twelve years;

it came to this that the girl was with child and the time came for the child to be born. That her father might hear no noise at all, the nurse brought brushwood and made with it a crackling fire: but later on what were they to do?

They hired an old woman and gave her the baby in a basket, and they covered the basket with roses and inside it they put a knife and a ring and a chain with a locket, all things which the prince had given the girl as gifts. To the old woman they said: 'Go you and cry aloud: Fair roses, fair roses for sale! and when anyone looks out from the palace, to him you must take the basket: leave it there and go away.' This the old woman did. The people in the palace took the roses from off the basket, and, lo! what did they see? They looked for the old woman; she was nowhere to be seen. Then the king issued a command that every woman and every girl should repair to the palace to sing a lullaby to the child: from this lullaby, he said, he would know who was the mother of the child. This order reached the tower, but the girl's father would not allow her to go to the palace. But it was a royal command, and in the end she too went. Every one sang a lullaby: not one of them in any way seemed to be the mother. Then the girl began her song:

Sleep, sleep, my baby, born
When they burned the crackling thorn.
Sleep, sleep, my baby, sold
With the rose for royal gold.

'This girl was the mother of the child.' They went and told her father. He said: 'What is written by Fate and by Christ, that no axe can do away.' The prince then married her, and they lived well and may we live yet better. Also I was there, and to me they gave a roll of bread and the dog with a short tail ate it up.

19

Luck and Good Sense

A PROBLEM always before a rustic philosopher is to try to see what guides human life to prosperity or to misery. Is it fate and the hidden decree of destiny? Is it pure chance, impersonal and mysterious? Is it a man's personal luck? What part is played by a man's own actions and character? The ideas of the Greeks on all these things are illustrated at length in the notes to No. 35 in *Forty-five Stories: A Man and his Luck.*

To these questions this story from Chios suggests the very reasonable and practical reply that though some men do seem lucky and others unlucky, nothing of much settled, permanent good can come to a man who has in himself no plain good sense: a real fool nothing can save or even profit.

In this story the common sense that came to the hero had clearly left the king, who swallowed the preposterous excuse the man gave to get out of his fix, that he had abstained from his bride to save the king's life, when he would obviously have been his heir and successor. But the Greeks like the sharp wit that gives a man the laugh, as they say in their own language, over his opponent.

NO. 19. LUCK AND GOOD SENSE[1]

There befell once a debate between Luck and Good Sense, Good Sense maintaining that apart from her nothing can avail a man; that if she is not there to aid a man, nothing can profit him. So the two came to an agreement: they would choose a man and over this man each of them would show her power. Luck began, giving him all the good things she had to give: all this time Good Sense withdrew herself from him.

One day this man was on a big farm ploughing, and on that very day it befell that two merchants passed that way;

[1] Unpublished text from Chios, recorded by Kanellakis.

their asses were loaded with goods of various kinds. As they were passing by they noticed the land where the man was ploughing; it was all covered with diamonds, and precious stones shining brightly. When the merchants saw this, they asked the man to let them gather up some of these stones; this, they told him, would clear the ground for his ploughing. The man was a fool and did not see what was up; indeed he begged them to clear the ground nicely for him, if they would be so good. So the two merchants gathered up stones and loaded their asses, and themselves as well. For all that, a whole pile of stones was left, and they had the idea of making the man himself take up a load and carry it to the city where they had their houses. So they told him this, and he left his oxen there to graze until he should come back, and the pile of stones he loaded on his shoulders.

As they were on their way the two merchants thought they would do well to keep the man with them, and to declare that all this treasure belonged to him, so that they might have no trouble with the king's government, which was well aware that they were only merchants and poor men. The man they would use as their own servant, and in this way it would be his back that would earn for them all the great bounties of God.

When they came to the city they told the man to take up his abode with them. They began work on a large scale and built a very big palace to live in, and told everyone that they were the man's secretaries: he was, they said, a very rich man but very haughty and would not condescend to go out and make acquaintance with other people.

After some time this came to the ears of the king. This king had a daughter, and his notion was that since there was such a very rich man in his realm it would be wise to make him his son-in-law, and not to go seeking anywhere else. So he sent for the two merchants who gave out that they were the man's secretaries, and asked them what this master of theirs was. They said that he was a very rich man but very haughty and would hold converse with no one, not even with the king himself. When the king heard all this, he again considered the matter and said to himself that when he had made him his son-in-law, then he and his daughter together would abate his pride and force him to speak to them in a fitting way.

When he had planned this, he told the secretaries that he wanted to make the man his son-in-law. They made their bow to the king to signify their agreement and told him that they would carry the matter through to a conclusion. Then, when the two came to their house, they told the man that they would arrange his marriage to the princess. So the marriage was celebrated with great pomp and magnificence.

In the evening the bride and the bridegroom were in their room together, and the groom went and lay down on one edge of the bed. The poor bride supposed that it was from modesty, and she too did the same. As dawn came near she came close to him and began talking, but he gave her a kick and pushed her out of the bed. She fell on her head on the floor, all covered with blood.

The princess went off crying with pain and came into the presence of the king. When he saw her covered with blood and crying, she told him how her husband had behaved to her. The king gave orders for men to go and take the bridegroom and hang him. But as they were on their way Good Sense came and took her place in the man's head. The man asked where he was being taken, and when he heard the king's intention, he asked if in that land there were laws. The men assured him that there were, and severe ones too. 'Well, then, since you have laws, why are you taking me off to be hanged before passing judgement on me?' This seemed to them reasonable, and they went back to the king and reported that he had said this. The king too found the man's saying reasonable, and he called for his vizier and the other people of the palace, and in the presence of them all he asked the man for what reason he had kicked his daughter and all but killed her. The man said in answer that before his marriage his Fate had one day appeared to him and told him that if he consorted with his wife on the first night of his marriage, the king would die and he himself take the kingdom. For this reason he had thought it better for the first night not to consort with his wife rather than to be with her and the king die. This therefore was why he had lain down at the edge of the bed away from his wife, and when at dawn she had come close to him he had been afraid that she would draw him to her wishes, and so he had acted in this way and given her a kick. He had sworn not to tell anyone of this until it was fully dawn, but he never expected that she would fall down and hit her head.

When the king heard all this he said that the man was in the right, and he thanked him for having saved his life, and proclaimed him as heir to his kingdom. So they lived happily and well and the man's wife with them.

Some time after all these things had come to pass, Luck and Good Sense met one another. Good Sense said to Luck: 'If it had not been for me, would not your man have today been dead? Without me all those friends of yours, those who depend on you, would all of them have come to nothing.'

20

The too lucky Man

THIS story from Thrace is, like Nos. 10 and 15, a story of the power of a parental blessing, in this case more potent than truly beneficent. It made a man so very lucky that he became uneasy and tried to break his run of luck by a transaction which could surely never bring him anything but loss; but to him even this turned out profitable, and in what was only a handful of dust he found the ring lost by the king of Egypt. At this point the story ends without any hint of subsequent disaster, such as befell Polykrates, the too fortunate tyrant of Samos who tried, but in vain, to break his luck by losing his valuable ring. Both in Herodotos' story and in our modern tale we have the Greek idea that too great prosperity may be a presage of misfortune. All through there is this feeling of the jealousy of the gods, the *φθόνος θεῶν*, what Norman Douglas has called their 'divine resentment.'

Just as the hero of our present story is persistently, and to his own feeling dangerously lucky, so we hear of men so naturally unlucky that nothing whatever can be done to help them. I adduce two stories of this sort: one from Thessaly, printed in *Laographia*, i. 668, and the other from Mytilene, in Kretschmer's *Der heutige lesbische Dialekt*, p. 536. In both of them an unlucky man went out to find this miserable Luck of his. He came to two fountains, of which one was no more than a dribble, while the other gushed out in abundance. The former, he was told, was his Luck; the other was the Luck of the king. The king then tried to help the man. In the story from Mytilene he gave him first a roast goose stuffed with gold: the man sold it for a song. Then he gave him a cake, in one half of which gold coins were hidden: this was the half of the cake the man casually gave away. Lastly the king gave him a golden apple; whatever he could throw it over should be his. The man threw the apple; it hit a wall and bounced back at him. The man was in his nature too unlucky for anything to turn out for his good. And the story from Thessaly is much the same.

In Greece lucky people are said to have 'a good hold', or 'a good step'—καλὸ χερικό, καλὸ ποδαρικό—whatever they set their hand to or enter upon prospers. And the opposite is of course 'a bad hold' or 'a bad step', expressions not so often heard because of the unpleasant words.

NO. 20. THE TOO LUCKY MAN[1]

There was once upon a time a young man; the poor fellow, when he was still very young, had lost his parents, and so was left an orphan, utterly an orphan. When his mother and his father were at the point of death, they called for him and said: 'My dear son, our time has come and we have to pass hence into the other world. We have nothing at all to leave you; neither cattle, nor sheep, nor vineyards, nor fields, nor anything else at all. Only we leave you this, our blessing: take up earth in your hands and it will turn to gold.' A few days after this they died. Having with him the blessing of his mother and of his father, whatever work the youth took in hand came to a flourishing end, so that it was a joy to behold: in a little while, from being a boy poor and of no account he became a young man full of favour and grace and very rich indeed. Had he not everything? Money and vineyards and fields, and sheep, and cattle, and houses? Anything else you can think of. He had more substance than anyone else in those parts.

Also he had a bosom friend, and one day he turned to him and said: 'My friend, I have something to say to you. Once I was a poor lad and much looked down upon. Now in this short time I have won all this wealth and all this honour. Whatever work I lay my hand to, it prospers. Where other men make losses and come to nothing, there I make profits past counting. What loss may mean I have up to now never known: the blessing of my parents guards me from harm. But this is not a matter which pleases me overmuch. I do not like this always making profits; I should like sometimes to have a loss. Indeed I am afraid that all this profit-making may bring upon me some great trouble. I think of this day and night and I can never be at peace. So I now beg you to give

[1] Text from Thrace, in *Arkheíon Thrakikoú . . . thisauroú*, ii. 173.

me your advice: what work can I undertake by which I may make a loss, for then my heart might be at rest.'

Then his friend turned and said to him: 'Well, my friend, since you ask me to tell how to make a loss, listen to this. Where do dates grow?' 'In Cairo.' 'Very well. Then if you wish to make a loss, this is quite enough. You don't need to burn a house, nor to invest money in Tunis; you need only buy all the dates there are in the market and load them on camels and take them to Cairo, and there try to sell them.'

This advice pleased the man. He went and bought up all the dates there were in that country and loaded them on camels and set out for Cairo. When he was near the city, it so happened that the king of Cairo had come out into the country with all his array and with his friends to sport with javelins. As the king was at this sport, he lost his wedding ring. He set all the soldiers at work to sieve the sand, but they could not find the ring. The king was thus grieved at heart, when he saw a long way off the young man of our story coming with his loaded camels. He sent two companies of men to summon the man with the camels. So the young man came up to the king and did reverence. The king asked him: 'From what country are you coming and what good things are you bringing us?' Then the young man said: 'O my king, and many be your years, I come from the regions of the White Sea [the Mediterranean] and am bringing you dates.' When the king heard that the man had come all the way from the White Sea to bring dates and sell them in Cairo, however sorry he was for him he could not keep himself from laughing, and said: 'You, my young man, must be a very silly fellow to bring dates here for sale when this is their own country. Now will you tell me; what have they cost you?' 'Seven piastres the oke,' said the youth. 'But here if you can't get them for half a piastre the oke they are skinning you.' 'Listen, my king, and many be your years, and I will tell you why I have brought dates here for sale. Although, my king, I may not have much brains, I am not altogether a fool. I was a lad with no money, and when my parents died they could leave me nothing but their blessing. But that blessing of my parents in a short while brought me to the winning of much substance and I became a very wealthy man, for whatever work I took in hand I always made a profit. What loss is I have up to this day never known. Yet—how can I put it?—this thing did not please me overmuch: I wanted to make a loss over some business, because I am afraid that some greater evil than that may come upon me. And for this reason I thought of bringing dates here to sell them and so to make a loss, seeing that this is the country where they grow. But all the same I think, my king, that even now I shall make no loss. For I am such a very lucky man that, well, this is what I mean: see, if I pick up from the ground even a little sand, in my hand it turns to gold.'

As he said this he picked up a little sand; he opened his hand and, Oh! what did he see? It was the king's ring which they had been looking for so long and in so many places, and all in vain. When the king saw it he was overjoyed that his ring had been found, and he turned to the youth and said: 'Unload your camels, and whatever merchandise you may have I will buy it all, and not for seven but for seventeen piastres the oke.' And in this way even then did the blessing of his parents protect the youth from loss.

21

St. George and the Dragon

As a rule, in Greece the ballads and the prose folktale narratives are in subject-matter kept strictly apart. But there are exceptions, and this story from Karpathos is one: in it we have the essentially ballad subject of St. George killing the dragon presented as a prose narrative in the folktale style, into which from time to time snatches of the ballad have been inserted as memory served. The lines are, however, not precisely as in any form of the ballad known to me, and no more in the Karpathos version than in any other. Numerous versions have been collected by Politis in *Laographía*, iv. 185, and one from Karpathos in Nouáros's volume *Dimotiká tragoúdia Karpáthou*, p. 277.

The prose redactor has done his work rather clumsily, and to add to the interest has worked in several incidents of Greek folktale which have no connexion whatever with St. George. Thus St. George's dogs belong properly to the story called *The three wonderful Dogs*, in *M.G.F.*, No. 28, a story possibly of Italian origin. The Jew with his false claim to have killed the monster refuted by the princess producing the tongues cut by the hero from the monster's heads is a commonplace found notably in the *Faithful John* group of stories; for which see *M.G.F.*, Nos. 36, 37; see also Stith Thompson's *Motif-Index*, H 105, 1.

It is remarkable that in the story local names of places in Karpathos have been introduced, and in this way the legend is presented as a local tradition. This is not very common in Greek folktales, and I am struck to find this same use of local names in several of the folktales from Karpathos printed by Mikhaïlídis-Nouáros.[1]

[1] Examples are in this author's *Laographiká sýmmeikta Karpáthou*, i. 272, 277, 292, 313. Two of these are in *M.G.F.*, pp. 62, 148.

NO. 21. ST. GEORGE AND THE DRAGON[1]

There was once, so the man told me, a village, and it had no water except from the spring; it had no well or anything else. Also by the spring there was a monster, and everyone had to satisfy it by offering it a child: it devoured one and then another. In this way it came to the turn of the princess. The king had one child only and her he refused to give.

And when they came to cast the lots,
  it fell upon the princess.
She was her father's only child,
  his one and only daughter.
'Come, deck my daughter as a bride,
  with all her fair adornments,
And send her to the lion's den,
  a present for his supper.'

But Saint George from Santorin was sorry for the king, and he came in a ship and with him were three dogs: one could break into a house, and one had the ears of a bear, and one was to guard the sheepfold. The saint, in the likeness of a man, went his way and so he came to the house of Balassáena. 'Good evening,' said he. 'And I am glad to see you.' 'I am now benighted, my good Christian woman, and I am a stranger here, and I don't know where to go to lodge.' The woman wanted to cook him something to eat. She blew her nose and then she spat to get moisture to knead the flour to make him some cakes. 'We have here, my dear Christian guest, we have here at our spring a monster, and if we do not send him a child to eat he will not let us fill our water jars.' 'I have had my dinner, my daughter, and have no need of anything.'

When night came all the houses were hung with black and all the ways were deserted. The man was astonished. 'What is all this business, my good daughter?' 'They are carrying away the king's daughter on her horse to give her to the monster to be devoured.' Then the man vanished from before her, and his dogs too. It was night, my dear child, and it was

[1] Text from Karpathos in *Laographiká sýmmeikta Karpáthou*, by Mikhaïlídis-Nouáros, i. 338.

all through the night that the monster devoured his victims. Before the girl dismounted, the saint came, and when she saw him, she said:

'O, flee from here, my stranger dear,
and take away your pitcher,
Lest now you die an evil death
and the monster come to eat you.'
'But I, my princess, have no fear,
and with my eyes I see him,
And with my ears I clearly hear
the footsteps of the monster.
So let me lie across your knee
And take a little slumber,
And when the monster shows himself,
tell me and I will waken.'
'So you were he who said to me
you have no fear of monsters,
And with your eyes can look at me,
and with your ears can hear me.'
From the girl's eyes the tears ran down;
fell on his cheek and waked him:
She was so full of fear she wept,
but not a word could utter.
Then up he stood to face the east,
and with the cross he signed him.
He smote the beast once with his lance,
and straight he cut his head off.

The monster, my dear child, had two heads. Then they climbed up on a wall, for the whole place was full of blood, running down like a river, all the way from the garden of Khanos. Then they went down to the spring and the girl brought him water. Then they cut off the heads of the monster. They cut out just the tongues and kept them safely, and the heads they left there.

'Now mount on your horse, my daughter, and go to your house and have no fear.' When the girl had recovered from her terror she turned and said to him: 'And what, my master, do you want of me when we are back in the village? Would you like to have Avlona or the land at Kilios? Whatever you please.' But after a long while he made answer:

> 'Tell him, if he will money spend,
> to build for me a chapel,
> And in the middle of the shrine
> to paint a man on horseback;
> A rider with his sword in hand
> and a long lance of silver.
> And if you die, or if you live,
> reveal my name to no man.'

Then they parted, and from Koúsoula he went the lower way and she the upper. Yet Saint George knew well that the girl would be attacked by a Jew who lived on the upper path. As she was passing in front of the Jew's house, he came out and saw her: 'What do you mean by coming back, for all the world to die of thirst?' She was much frightened and said to him: 'A man has killed the monster. But who he was I do not know.' Then the Jew seized the bridle and drew her into his courtyard. 'You must say that it was I who killed him, when the monster was ready to devour you. If you won't, I'll kill you.' So the girl swore that she would say this. In the king's palace they were all lamenting, fit to kill themselves, when, behold, the girl appeared, and following her the Jew. 'O, my daughter, you who are my daughter, my dear daughter, come, my daughter, and tell us what has happened to you. We thought you were lost to us.' 'Behold, this is the Jew who killed the monster and saved me.' 'Then we must baptize him, my daughter, and give him to you as your husband.' So they baptized the Jew and married them, and that evening they set the tables and all the rest of it; a marvel to behold.

After the marriage the girl called her father to come out into the courtyard, and said to him: 'This is not the man, my dear father, who delivered me. He was a stranger with three dogs as big as calves, and I know him well, because when he killed the monster I plunged my hand in the blood and pressed it up against his back. Look now and see if you can find him, and let me have him as my husband.' Then the king made a proclamation: all and every dog in the village must be brought together, and all the cats too, to be at the wedding. The woman Balassáena came to the wedding and they saw that she was hiding a piece of meat inside her dress. 'What is this which you are hiding and going off with?' 'I have a little cat, my dears, and I am taking it for him to eat.' 'Very well then; let us go and see your cat.' They went, and in her house they found a man who shone as brightly as the sun. 'And what is your name?' 'I am called George.' Then they got ready instruments of music to make an escort for him. 'Be careful; I have some dogs with me who will not endure ill treatment, and they would break up the banquet. If you want me, let us make an agreement that whatever my dogs do, no one will breathe a word.' So they went off together.

When the girl saw him she recognized him at once. They gave him a chair and he sat down. They set before him meat to eat and fish of the most royal kind. Then the cup came round to him. He rose up to give a blessing and said: 'Boys, long live the king.' The housebreaker dog picked up a bowl with cakes in it and like lightning threw it at the Jew, who was all smeared with it. The king with his sword rose up and cried aloud: 'Peace be with you.' No one said a word. Saint George gave another blessing: 'Boys, long live the queen.' Then the dog with bears' ears picked up a bowl and again attacked the Jew and broke the bowl on him. 'Be silent; make him sit down here just as he is.' Then they gave the Jew ten and ten and one little stroke more just for luck. The king was beside himself with delight. He sent off his daughter to fetch the monster's heads from where she had hidden them. When the heads were laid out there and displayed in the palace, Saint George said to the Jew: 'You unbaptized creature, where are the tongues that belong to these heads?' Then the saint produced the tongues and cast them down there alongside of the heads: tongues as big as a cow's. Then they took the Jew outside and set him alight with petrol.

O you, my saint, my holy George,
how shall I sing your praises?
You who have killed the monster snake,
the plague of all our country.

Who in our land deep in a well
 at every dawn and evening
Would have a child, and if we failed
 to bring to him his supper,
No one to save the land from thirst
 could draw a drop of water.

Saint George then disappeared asking neither payment nor anything else. And the next Sunday they made a fine wedding for the princess, and the village was set free from its troubles.

22

The Robber Captain

THIS story of a girl who kills all but one of a band of forty robbers, or ogres, and then escapes the vengeance of the one whom she has just failed to kill, belongs seemingly to the eastern part of the Greek world, for it is from here that all the as yet recorded variants come. We have the following:

1. The present text from Vatka near Kyzikos, in *Mikrasiatiká Khroniká*, v. 207.
2. CAPPADOCIA: *M.G. in A.M.*, p. 342.
3. MYTILENE: Kretschmer, *Der heutige lesbische Dialekt*, p. 502.
4. THRACE: in *Thrakiká*, xvii. 166.
5. CYPRUS: Sakellarios, *Kypriaká*, ii. 301.
6. ASTYPÁLAIA: *Forty-five Stories*, p. 94.

The version from Cyprus is rather divergent; it has no mention of the killing of the robbers, or ogres, and the place of the cruel husband is taken by a corpse-eating ghoul, the Three-eyed One, *ὁ Τρίμματος*. The Astypálaia version is a good deal spun out by an account of how the girl bamboozled a foolish ogre called Master Parsley, and ends up by her being rescued from a cave, in which the ogre has shut her up to suck her blood, by the familiar Three Gifted Champions. The principal contacts with other stories are this one with the Gifted Champions, who properly belong to one of the sub-stories in *The Silent Princess*, for which see *M.G.F.*, p. 323, and *Folklore*, lxiii. 129, and the coaxing of the ogre to his destruction, which belongs to a class of stories of how clever girls get the better of the proverbially foolish ogres: an example from Thrace is in *Thrakiká*, xv. 358. The reader may be referred to Halliday's discussion of the present story in *M.G. in A.M.*, p. 248.

That the heroine at the end makes herself known to the king by a beautiful piece of embroidery, which shows a special knowledge of the king and of the interior of his palace, is an episode which does not really fit well with the rest of the story, and I take it that its presence is to be explained by outside influence. There is a whole set of stories in which at the end the ill-used heroine gathers together an audience and by telling them all her misfortunes is recognized and the villain punished. This incident is particularly in place in *The Girl who was left at Home*, for which see *M.G.F.*, p. 367. It is common also in the story of *The three Oranges*, in *M.G.F.*, No. 1. In two versions of this latter story, the one translated in *M.G.F.* and the one printed by Kamboúroglou, p. 19, the girl does not tell a story but reveals herself by working all her adventures into a piece of embroidery, and in this way bringing about her recognition. This pretty episode has been picked up and neatly fitted into our story.

The version I have here printed was recorded quite recently from a refugee from the village of Vatka in the district of Kyzikos. In the article from which I take it, printed in the *Mikrasiatiká Khroniká*, we are told that the dialect of this village is quite incomprehensible to other Greeks, and this I can well believe; indeed, without the notes provided I should not have been able to make a translation of it at all, and even so I cannot be quite certain that in some phrases small errors may not have crept in. From a short study of the dialect by Mr. Thanasi Kostakis we learn that it is a variety of Tsakonian, brought to the district of Kyzikos by people from the Peloponnese; the date is uncertain but can, it seems, hardly have been earlier than the seventeenth century.[1] With the dispersal of the refugees from Vatka the dialect must by now be as good as dead. Did they bring the story with them from Tsakonia, or pick it up in Anatolia?

NO. 22. THE ROBBER CAPTAIN[2]

Once upon a time there was a king, and he had no children. The years went on; the king grew old and the queen too. One day the king said to the queen: 'My wife, we have grown old, and we have no heir: What are we to do? I will go my way to find some doctor to help us, and so we may have an heir.'

The king went off. As he was on the way he met an angel, though he did not know it was an angel: he thought it was a man. The angel said to the king: 'My lord king, where are you going?' The king said to the angel: 'How do you know

[1] This study forms the second part of Kostakis's Tsakonian Grammar, *Σύντομη γραμματική τῆς Τσακωνικῆς διαλέκτου*, published at Athens in 1951 by the Institut français d'Athènes.

[2] Text from Vatka near Kyzikos; printed in *Mikrasiatiká Khroniká*, v (1942), p. 207.

that I am a king?' 'I know that you are a king. I also know why you are making this journey; you want to find a doctor that by his help you may have a child to be your heir. Come, my lord king: now go back to your village, to your city, to your palace, and you shall have a daughter. But this daughter, until she is twenty years old, must never look upon anyone except you and her mother and her teacher.'

The king went back to his city, and after nine months the queen had a little daughter: until she was fifteen years old she never set eyes upon anyone except her father and her mother and her teacher. The king built a tower, setting it in the midst of the sea; it had no door; it had only a window, and above the window there was a sword, hanging there suspended. Inside the tower there was a mirror so that the girl could in it see the whole world.

A robber, an outlaw, who had a company of forty young men, heard that the king had a very fair daughter who had never looked upon anyone. This robber said: 'We will go and carry off this girl.' The robbers came, and outside the king's city they met an old man. The captain asked this old man: 'Where does the king keep his fair daughter?' The old man said: 'The king has built a tower in the midst of the sea, and in it is his fair daughter with her teacher.' The robber said to one of his young men: 'It is you who must go and carry off this girl.' The young man went into a boat and went to the tower. He looked this way and he looked that way, but he could not find a door; he saw only a window. The girl in her mirror saw that a man had pushed his head in through the window. She pressed the button; down fell the sword and cut off the robber's head. His head fell inside the tower and his body fell down into the sea.

And so it came about that the youth did not come back again; so the captain said: 'Why doesn't the man come back? Can he have gone there and be now taking his pleasure so that he has forgotten about coming back?' Then a second youth went; he looked at the tower this way and that way, and he too found that there was no door, so he pushed his head in at the window. The sword fell and cut off his head. Not to make too long a story of it, the same thing happened to all the forty youths: the girl cut off the head of every one of them.

Then said the captain: 'What has happened to them? All of them going and not coming back again? There is something going on: I must go and see for myself.' The captain went; he looked this way and he looked that way; he could hear nothing. Then he looked at the window and pushed his head in just a little way. The sword fell, but did no more than cut a little hair off the crown of his head. Then said the captain: 'What can you be up to, you bitch?' He ran off and took a warship and went to the city of the king. Next day the king went to the tower to visit his daughter. He looked at the heads which his daughter had cut off and said: 'I must take my daughter away from here. What I see here is no good thing.' So he took the girl and went off to the palace.

Next day at dawn the king saw a warship in his harbour. He ordered the harbour master to go to see what ship it was. So the harbour master went and inquired. The captain said to him: 'I am the son of the King of the Sea,' and he set before him a banquet with many fine dishes, and they ate and drank. Then the harbour master went back to the king and said: 'This man is the son of the King of the Sea.' Next day the king went down to bid him welcome, and the man made a great feast, and they ate and drank and had very good entertainment. The king said to the captain: 'You must come to my palace that the queen may see you, and so we can eat and drink together.'

Next day the captain went to the king's palace, and while they were eating and drinking the queen was very well pleased with the young captain; then she said to the king: 'Let us make this man our son-in-law.' The king said: 'My wife, to make sure that no evil will come upon her, three more years must pass before the girl can come out into the world.' The queen answered: 'Let us take the youth and marry him to our daughter; then we can let the three years pass and after that let her go freely out into the world.' So they called for the boy: 'We love you well and want to make you our son-in-law. You can live here for three years and get three children, and after that you can go to your own country and later on come back to us again.' The young man said: 'As you wish, so let it be done.'

With much feasting and drinking the pair were crowned in marriage, and they stayed in that country for three years, and had three children. The bridegroom never let out a word about his not being the son of a king.

One day later on he privily, all by himself, wrote a letter, and gave it to the captain he had with him and said: 'To-morrow at dawn you are to come here and hand me this letter.' Next day the man came and handed him the letter. The bridegroom read the letter, the letter he had himself written, and smote his knees in horror. The king asked him what letter it was, and what was the matter. 'My father the king is sick and on the point of death.' 'Oh, my lad, you must go and visit your father; write me a letter about it all.' The man then rose up and took his wife and his children and embarked and went off. When he was on board he said to his wife: 'And now what will you be up to, you bitch, now that I have got you?' He shut up his wife and his children down below in the cabin, and then he turned his guns against the palace and reduced it to ashes.

Then the ship sailed on and on for forty days until they came to the foot of a great wooded mountain; there he had his house. The man took a ship's boat and brought his children and his wife ashore, and to her he said: 'Take the children off and be quick.' The wife was so much frightened that she could not run, and the children were small. Then he seized the children by the hair and cut off their heads. In this way he killed all the three of them. Then he said to his wife: 'Now we must go off, and quickly.' They went into a wood, deep and wild. He seized his wife and said to her: 'Now I mean to kill you.' She started crying.

He seized her and tied her feet and hanged her up on a tree. Then he went off to collect wood, to lay it beneath her and make a fire and burn her. She began to cry: 'Oh! what are you doing?' The robber searched in his pocket to find matches to light the fire; he had none; he had forgotten and left them in the ship. So he left her hanging there while he went off to his village to get some matches to light the fire.

As she was hanging there and crying, some camels passed by. They were laden with bales of cotton. The camel-drivers heard someone on the hill crying and one of them said: 'Who can this be crying? We must go and look.' They went to the place and found a girl hung up by her feet. They asked her: 'How do you come to be hanged up here? Who has hung you up?' The girl said: 'Oh! let me loose.' So they untied the girl. The men went to where the camels were and unloaded a bale of cotton; they hid the woman inside it and went their way. The robber came back and found the girl was not there. He saw that camels had passed by and he ran and overtook them and said to the drivers: 'The girl whom you took away from here; what have you done with her?' 'We have seen no girl at all. Search all the bales of cotton and make quite sure.' The robber examined all the bales of cotton and found them from the outside all just cotton; all quite soft; nothing solid. Then he went back again into the wood, and looked here and looked there; but he could find nothing. He went also to the town where the camel-drivers had gone to search there.

Outside the walls of the town the camel-drivers met an old man; he had three daughters and the drivers said to him: 'We found this girl in the wood and a robber had hung her up from a tree by her feet to burn her. We took the girl and now have her with us. Now if we take her into the town, people will see her and the man will find out and come here to carry her away. We would like to leave her here with your daughters; she can work for you, and you can give her a morsel of bread to eat.' The old man said: 'You may leave her here.' The camel-drivers went off about their business.

These girls used to be given pieces of cloth by the king for them to embroider. This girl with them as a guest was very well instructed in the art of embroidery: in fact she embroidered very beautifully. She said to the other girls: 'Let me too do some of the embroidery.' Then one day the stranger, without the others seeing her, took a piece of cloth and in a room all by herself worked an embroidery on it. She worked on it in embroidery the king on his terrace and all his palace as well. Then privily she put this cloth into the basket with all the other embroideries. The youngest girl took the basket and carried it to the palace. The king looked at all the embroideries one after the other, and in this piece he recognized himself on his terrace and all his palace as well. He asked the girl: 'Who was it who embroidered this cloth?' The girl said: 'It was my sister.' 'Go and call for your sister, the one who embroidered this cloth.' The girl went and called for her. The girl came, and the king asked her: 'Was it you who embroidered this cloth?' 'No; it was my sister.' The king called for her too and asked: 'Was it you who embroidered this cloth?' The girl would not tell a lie but told him the truth. 'My lord king, one day some camel-drivers left in our house a girl; a robber had tied her up in the wood and was going to burn her. Since then she has been in our house with us. This is the girl who embroidered the cloth.' The king said: 'That girl I wish to take as my wife.'

The sisters went and told the girl: 'The king wants to take you for his wife.' The girl said: 'I will take him, only don't let the robber find out and come and carry me away.' The marriage was then made and the king took the girl for his wife. A little while afterwards the robber found out that the girl had been hidden in the old man's house, and that from there the king had taken her to be his wife. The robber went to the old man and asked him: 'Why did you tell me lies and keep the girl hidden away?' What answer could the old man make? Then the robber took the old man and his three daughters and killed them; he meant then to go to the palace, to take his wife and murder her.

The man went and put on an officer's uniform and went in at the door of the palace. The soldiers saw him, but they said nothing and he passed in. He was about to go up the staircase when he saw two lions, one on this side and one on that; he could not pass. He turned back and went to the butcher and from him he took two lambs; he gave one lamb to one lion and the other to the other, and so he passed on right inside. He managed to go right into the room where the king slept at night with the queen. There he saw the queen by the side of the king. He seized her by the hand and pulled her towards him, saying: 'Come here.' The queen saw an officer in uniform and made no answer. The officer lifted her up in his arms and went out. They were on their way to go down the staircase, he pushing the woman before him. The lions knew the queen and did not attack her, but the robber had scarcely passed when she cried out to the lions: 'Catch that man.' Then the two lions seized him and tore him to pieces.

The wife turned to go back through the gate. She met her husband and he said: 'My wife, what has happened to you? Where were you? I saw in my dream that someone came and seized you but where he took you I do not know.' Then said the queen: 'Look at the lions; see who they are devouring.'

23

The Herb of Love

A STORY which I have called *The Girl who was left at Home* is under the number 57 discussed in *M.G.F.* It is a story widely spread in the Balkans and perhaps originally Turkish. The references there given will show that it has been printed three times in English, but it will be convenient to give here a brief outline of the narrative. A man with a daughter found himself obliged to go abroad, and he left his daughter in the charge of a man who presently proved to be a villain and assaulted her. The girl escaped and was married. Later on she was again attacked by the same villain. She then dressed as a boy, and in the typical form of the story made her living by making and selling the Turkish sweetmeat called halvá, a kind of toffee. For this reason Kunos has called the Stambul version *Das schöne Helva Mädchen*, and Halliday in his study of the story in *M.G. in A.M.*, uses the title *The beautiful Girl Sweetmeatmaker.* At the end of the story the girl gathered an audience together and narrated her sufferings, and denounced the villain, who was then punished.

Anyone who reads the present Pontic story, which I have called *The Herb of Love*,[1] will see that it is a novel, a love story, based on the folktale, *The Girl who was left at Home.* In *The Herb of Love* the girl is left in the charge of a moneychanger, and he is the villain of the story. The second attack upon the heroine is made through the bird who is his servant and helper and, as far as the girl is concerned, his double. The bird is really, to use the language of witchcraft, his familiar spirit, knowing where the body was buried and carrying to it the girl's bag of pearls. The city to which the body of the moneychanger is carried by the sea and to which the boy goes in pursuit of the bird is, I think, Constantinople, to the Greeks the city *par excellence*, called here 'the great city'.

Like all these novels *The Herb of Love* seems to be found in one place only—no doubt where it was first constructed. There are other examples of the building of a novel on the foundation of a folktale. In *Forty-five Stories*, No. 32, *The Boatman* is modelled on the tale *Which succeeds best? Truth or Lies?* and in this book I have

[1] In his text Papadópoulos uses the title *The wealthy Boy*, τὸ πλουσιόπαιδον.

pointed out that No. 10 has behind it the story of *The Son of the Hunter*. And I cannot but suspect that No. 24 in this book, *The two Pauls*, has been developed from a folktale about two men, perhaps brothers, who were in appearance identical.

But this relation of our story to a folktale hardly exhausts its interest. We must ask what is the significance of some of the episodes in this tale of the stormy passage of a youth and a girl from their sheltered lives in their parents' houses—and in both cases this is heavily stressed—to their final happiness in the Pastures of the Sun. It is to be noted that as they are to be lovers it was in submission to the will of the boy that the girl started for the Pastures, on the way to which they came to the spring where the Herb of Love chanced to be. The girl was reluctant and wanted to go to the place where in earlier years she had gone with her mother: that is, to remain in her maiden state. In the brother- and sister-relationship in these stories it is typical that the sister takes the lead; that here she yields to the boy is a sign that their earlier relationship is changing to the feeling of love, and this change is marked by their coming to the flowery spring of refreshment and rest, sheltered beneath the high windy ridge of the mountain. Here grew the flower which I venture to call the Herb of Love, which when the girl was left she took as a guide to find her way to her lover; which also, at the end of the story, brought happiness again by restoring the sight of the two blind old mothers.

The heroine of the folktale, *The Girl who was left at Home* was twice attacked by the villain. So is the girl in this story: first by the moneychanger, who breaks up her maiden life in her father's house, and the second time, when the bird brought about the loss of her lover. Both attacks are remedied by the herb: it acts as her guide when she goes off from the spring to find her lover, and it helps her sorrowing parents by restoring her mother's eyesight. Thus in the Pastures the heroine can live happily both as a wife and as a daughter.

Taken in this way the sheltered spring with its cool water is a figure of the awakening of love; the Pastures of the Sun are the place of lasting and settled happiness, for the older as well as for the younger pair. These high pastures of the Pontic country, the *parkhária*, have a great attraction for the Greeks of the land, who have to live in the hot cities of the coast. In other ways too the story is made more effective. The lovers begin their common life in the mire and squalor of the Turkish burial ground; they finally reach the beautiful upland pastures. The girl's wealth is in pearls and gems; the moneychanger's in the more prosaic form of hard cash.

And lastly, why does the placing at its root of the jars of treasure make the poplar grow withered and hollow? If we turn to No. 35 in *Forty-five Stories*, *The Man and his Luck*, we shall see that a pot of gold at its root made a tree turn yellow and withered. I have given there other examples, but can give no solution: can it be that the yellowness of the gold makes the tree also yellow?

NO. 23. THE HERB OF LOVE[1]

So the story went on and on, and there was once a boy of great wealth. He was an only son and his father and his mother watched over him well: on him let no rain, let no snow ever fall! Green branches of palm were ever about him, nor was he allowed at any time to go away from his home. He grew up and became a handsome youth. The boys who were with him went off to foreign lands and came home again, young men carrying weapons, while he never went outside the village. He used to gaze at boys of his own age telling stories of the fine things to be seen abroad, and he found them strange and wonderful. Every time he was with the boys he heard tell of things of which even in his dreams he could get no sight.

Saying nothing to his parents about it, he formed a plan to go abroad with the other boys of his company. He begged that the next time they went they would take him with them, and he promised them a little money to say nothing about it to his father or his mother. But one boy was careless and without intending it let out the secret. His father and mother heard of it and were much troubled. He was their one and only son and how could they part with him? And what could he do if he did go abroad? Had they not money to live on? He had no need to go and make money to bring them. This trouble gave them no rest; up and down all the time! 'As for me,' his mother would say, 'never will I let my son leave my arms. To the devil with all this nonsense! It has sent my son

[1] Text from Stavrí in Pontos; printed in *Arkheion Pontou*, xii. 183.

out of his mind.' Then said the father: 'Wife, don't be afraid. I will never let him go. I know what is to be done.'

Secretly he sent for the boys who were to go abroad, and gave each of them a gold piece, and asked them to make their departure quietly that his son might not see them. And what could the travellers want more than this? They took the money and one night went off without anyone knowing of it. When the young man heard of this, he was very angry with them, and with his father even angrier. He rose up one night when it was near dawn and took some money from his father's purse; packed up his clothes and went off on the first road handy: he was set on going abroad. So he walked on and walked on until the evening, and when it was evening he lay down and slept; in the morning he went on his way again. In five days he came to the city. It had become dark and in that place there was a Turkish burial ground; he went into it. 'Here I will rest,' said he, 'and in the morning I will go down into the city.' He went into a little hole dug in the ground without knowing that it was being used for burying dead men: there he lay down. But in such a place how could he sleep? He waited for the dawn, and then he would get up and go down into the city.

In that city there was a rich lord: he had much wealth and was the master of many ships; he was also a fine ship's captain. He used to make long voyages, going and coming and bringing back with him much gold coin, jewels, and pearls. There was also there a moneychanger who was his close friend; he used to let him have all the fine things he brought back with him, and he would sell them. The time came when he would start on a very long voyage and he was taking his wife with him. He had also an only daughter, but her he did not take with him on the journey. At that time there were pirates on the sea and he was afraid that something might happen to their darling. He entrusted his daughter and all his house to the moneychanger and went off. The moneychanger was always in and out of the rich man's house, keeping guard over it. Also he looked after the girl to see that nothing happened to her, and that no one did her any harm. He managed the whole business as if he were master of the house and her own father, and the girl for her part was very well pleased and quite happy. That her father and her mother were away was no trouble to her at all. In this way, for some time they went on very well.

One evening the moneychanger tried to beguile the girl. She shouted and cried and would not let him come near her; she was afraid that he would be robbing her of the pearls she had. You see that her mother, when she was to start on her journey, knew what might happen to her daughter, and she took some human hair and wove it into what was like a little bag. This she filled with her fine jewels and her pearls, and twisted it into the girl's hair and hid it under her plaits. 'My little daughter,' said she, 'keep this hidden; some time it will be of use to you.'

The moneychanger had never heard anything of the pearls and jewels; his intentions had been quite other, but the girl had fully and finally rebuffed him; he was also afraid that her father might come and she tell him of it. So he took out a knife and stabbed her with it. The girl was so much frightened that she fainted, and the man thought that she was dead. He took a sack and put her into it and tied up the mouth of the sack. When the dawn was near he took the sack and carried it to the graveyard, burying it in an empty grave; then he went away. He went and stole the rich man's goods and valuables and carried them away to his own house. Then he stuffed people up by saying that the sea captain's house had been pillaged and that his daughter had disappeared. And this people believed: 'Never', they said, 'would the moneychanger have done such a thing to his friend.'

Now let us go and see what had become of the rich young man. When the dawn came, he heard a noise and saw a man coming with something loaded on his back. The man came and stood close to where he was, and set down what had been on his back and dragged it into another little hole; digging into the earth with a pick, he covered it up. Then the man threw the pick aside and left it there. The boy was so much frightened that he crouched down where he was, afraid to draw a breath. He waited for some time and then stood up and looked all round: the place was empty; not a soul; not a sound. 'I will stay here,' said he, 'until it is fully dawn, and then I will get up and go off.' When he had said this, he heard a groaning. He jumped up; he listened, and the groaning was coming from the place where the man had dug. He went to the place and pushed the earth aside and brought out a sack with its mouth tied up. He opened the sack and what did he see? A beautiful girl, lying as if she were dead, stabbed with a knife, and groaning deeply. He took her out from the sack and pulled away the knife. The blood began to flow and the boy took out his kerchief and bound up the wound. Near by, there was some water. Cupping his hands, he brought water and washed away the blood a little. He chafed her hands and her feet and poured water over her face, and, not to make a long story of it, he made her open her eyes. When day dawned she had quite come to herself. She rose up and shook off the earth and washed away all the blood and set herself a little in order. The boy looked at her as one filled with astonishment, nor could he ever stop asking her where she came from and how she had suffered this mishap. But she made him no answer at all. She took the sack, rolled up the knife in it, and put it under her arm. Then she turned and looked into the boy's eyes and said: 'Up! Come with me, and I conjure you to say nothing to anyone of this matter.'

They went down to the city, and she knew all the ways and alleys in it; they rented a very small house at the edge of the city and in it they lived. She sent the boy out to buy whatever was needed for the furnishing of the little house. All the outside business was done by the boy; the girl never went abroad at all and was seen by nobody. The boy loved her as though she had been his sister, and whatever she told him he did. She sent him out to buy all their fine food and furnishings, and they ate and drank and lived there like brother and sister: she used to call him 'my little brother,' and he used to call her 'my little sister.' Up and down, it was always 'my little sister.' The boy had their little fortune in his hands and in paying their expenses he was reckless; for every once they paid twice. The report of this went abroad, and the shopkeepers one may say milked them.

When spring came the boy's little store of money was exhausted. When the girl heard this she said to him: 'Don't be vexed that your money has come to an end; don't let this trouble you. If your money has come to an end, then we can begin living on mine.' The boy thought this very strange and said to himself: 'She must be mocking me; where can she keep this money of hers that I never see it?' 'Come then; undo my plaits,' said the girl, 'and among them there is a little bag woven of hair; bring it out. Be careful and notice how it is twisted among my plaits, and then you can put it back in place again.' The boy very carefully undid the plaits and brought out the little bag. The girl took it and opened it and let him see the jewels and the pearls; it was the first time the boy had seen such things. The girl took out one pearl; the rest she put back again among her hair. The pearl she gave to the boy, saying: 'Go right down to the shore, and there you will find a moneychanger; sell him the pearl and bring back the money.' The boy took it and went down to the moneychanger. 'What do you want, my lad?' said the moneychanger. 'I have a pearl to sell; will you buy it?' said the boy. The moneychanger took the pearl and looked at it, and he longed to have it. 'Well, boy, shall I pay you in gold pieces or will you have silver?' 'If you can, my uncle, give it me all in silver,' said the boy. He wanted small money, so that when he went to the market he might have no difficulty about changing money.

The moneychanger brought him out a bag of silver coins. When the boy saw the bag he changed his mind; he wished he had asked for gold pieces; he was thinking how he could carry all that money. The moneychanger was a clever man and understood this: 'Don't trouble yourself,' he said to the boy. 'I will send my servant to carry the money to your house,' for indeed he wanted to find out where the boy's house was. The boy in front and behind him the servant loaded with the money went off to the house. The boy was now once more full of cheer and spent money to a great amount. The moneychanger sold the pearl and got the double for it. He did not know where the pearl came from and he became very uneasy; further, he was afraid of it being found out what he had done to the girl, and that would be his ruin.

The rich man, the ship's captain, and his wife came back from their voyage. They found out what had happened to their house and for this nothing could console them. The moneychanger told them that one evening he had gone to the house and found the doors and windows all standing open; everything had been stolen and the girl had disappeared. This was the story he told to satisfy them, and they believed it: their distress was so great that what to do they knew not. They locked up their house and went to look for their child.

As soon as the girl's father and mother had gone off, the moneychanger was no longer in any fear; his great curiosity was to find out where the boy had got the pearl. He set up a great friendship with him and every time he came across him in the market he used to take him off to the best taverns there; they would eat and drink and all the costs were at the charge of the moneychanger. He carried him off to his house and paid him the greatest attention.

By such devilish tricks as these the moneychanger tried to find out from the boy how the pearl had come into his hands. But how to find this out? The boy had taken an oath, and he would never say a single word about the girl or about what she had. One day the boy, the Son of Wealth, said to the girl: 'This man has been very kind to us and has a great value for me. He takes me off to eat and drink with him; he invites me to his house and treats me most honourably. We on our side ought to do something. Let me just ask him to come to our place; he can dine here with me in our house.' The girl consented and said: Tomorrow in the morning, you go down into the market and buy whatever provisions are needed and ask him to come here in the evening. By the time you come, everything shall be ready. Set the table and you can eat and drink. Wine too you can give him in plenty; he is very fond of wine. Only when the time comes for the rice to be served you must let me know, for me to bring it in myself.

Next day in the evening the moneychanger came to their house. The boy received him well and they sat down to table: there was food, and drink in abundance; they ate and drank and diverted themselves. The wine also was good. The moneychanger drank and went on drinking. The drink mastered him and he began to talk at random. They ate of all the dishes and then came the time for the rice to be served. The boy made a sign to the girl, and she on her side was all ready. She took a little dish and put the rice on it, taking it up with her left hand. Underneath the dish with her right hand she held the knife with which the moneychanger had stabbed her. She entered the room where they were, and as she set the rice on the table she drove the knife into the moneychanger's heart. 'Ah!' said he, and fell down off his stool; after a short struggle his soul departed. The boy in dismay rose up to speak. 'Say nothing,' said the girl. 'Run and look for a porter and bring him here.' The boy ran off for the porter, and she put the dead body of the moneychanger into the very sack which she had brought with her from the graveyard, and tied up its mouth. She washed all the blood away and cleared the table. Then she dragged the sack away and set it outside in the courtyard. The boy came up and with him the porter. They gave him a bag of silver and loaded him with the sack and told him to take it and throw it into the sea. The porter did as they told him and then went his way. The girl had had her revenge and was very well pleased. The boy, the Son of Wealth, was much disturbed in his mind; he was pale from fear and lost all his cheerfulness. 'Well now, my little brother,' said the girl, 'I will tell you the story of my troubles, but you must say nothing to anybody and what I bid you you must do.' Then she told him about her father and her mother and about their life and their journeys and their friendship with the moneychanger and his dishonourable doings. When she told him of her last trouble, she was even in tears. For her sake the boy was even more grieved; he comforted her and swore with an oath to do whatever she told him to do.

When this trouble was all over, they were at ease and lived happily as at first; there was nothing of which they had need. Very often they felt that they remembered their parents with longing and this was a bitterness to them. They had hope in

God that no evil would happen to them; in such a hope they passed their days. May came to an end and the hot weather was upon them, and it became no longer possible for them to remain in the town. All the people were leaving and going up to the high ground and to the mountain pastures. They too resolved to go. The girl wanted to go to the place where in earlier years she used to go with her mother, but the boy did not wish this. He wanted to go to the Pastures of the Sun which lay close to their village, and to this the girl consented: to whatever one of them said the other never said No. They bought plenty of provisions and made everything ready. They engaged muleteers and started off for the Pastures of the Sun. They went a long way across the level ground and then they crossed a bridge and struck into a lofty range of hills. They were hardly half way up the mountain when evening came on. They halted and in the morning went on up to the ridge. Both they and their horses were tired but they could not remain there: the ridge was very high and a heavy wind thrashed against it. They turned their horses heads and went to a place much lower down. There was in that place a little spring of water, of cold water. They unpacked the loads and rested there. The servants went to graze the horses and the boy and the girl stayed there with the luggage close by the spring. As they were talking together, the girl was tired and became sleepy; she leaned up against the boy and so fell asleep. To pass the time he undid her plaits and brought out the little bag with the jewels in it to count them; his idea was to see how many bags of silver they came to.

When he had counted them over once and again, he put them back into the little bag and straightened the girl's hair again to put the bag back in its place. How he did it I don't know, but the little bag slipped from his hands. As he was reaching out his hand to take it again, there came a monstrous big bird and snatched up the bag and was off. The boy very gently laid the girl down on the grass and started to run in pursuit of the bird. The bird was flying very low and he ran on to catch it. He ran now this way and now that, but he could never catch the bird. Chasing after it he came down to the city, and still the bird did not perch. It flew on, and passing low it went out over the sea. The boy got into a boat and followed after it. He chased it until they came to another city—the Great City. Wherever he saw the bird go he pursued it, but inside the city he lost it. He did not see where it went and he never saw it any more. Then he wanted to go back again, but he was not given permission. To get this permission he had to conform to the custom of the city; himself and with his own hands to plant a vine and to take of its fruit and offer it to the ruler of the city. If the ruler were satisfied, then he would grant the permission. The boy, the Son of Wealth, lost no time: he planted a vine and there he waited for it to bear grapes. Day and night he thought of the girl, saying: 'And what may chance to have befallen my little sister? And now,' thought he, 'her pearls have been stolen; they've gone right off with them.' Such were his thoughts as he sat there eating out his heart.

The bird which had snatched the little bag and gone off with it had been the property of the moneychanger, who had bought it somewhere and kept it in a cage. Every day when he went to bring the bird its food he used to say: 'Ah, my little bird; you know where the boy keeps the pearls. I wish you would tell me.' The bird would then make a sign, bowing its head down. As soon as the moneychanger disappeared, some people said he had been killed, others said that he had gone on a voyage; no one really knew what had happened to him. The bird knew the whole matter. It knew the base doings of the moneychanger, what he had done and what had happened to him, and how the waves had carried his dead body as far as the Great City. Also the bird knew where the jewels and the pearls were to be found.

Ever since the death of the moneychanger the bird in its grief never ate anything any more. The people in the house were sorry for it and lest it should die of hunger they opened the cage and let it go free. The bird had followed after the boy and the girl and watched its chance to take the little bag with the pearls. And as we have already said, close by the little spring of water it snatched the bag away. It had then gone to the Great City to find the body of the moneychanger; to him it would give the bag.

When it came to the Great City the bird was very tired. It came upon three tall poplar trees, all hollow from the top to the root. On the middle of the three trees the bird perched and there came to rest. Inside the tree there were multitudes of ants and they gnawed at the bird's feet. At this the bird lowered its head to kill the ants; it was confused and unclasped its talons. Oh, oh, oh! the little bag fell down inside the hollow poplar, down, down to its roots. The bird saw that it could not get the bag up again and in great distress flew off, leaving it there. It was there at the root of the poplar tree that the body of the moneychanger had been buried; even dead the man kept piling up money. Three jars he had filled with treasure and brought them there and laid them at the root of the poplar. It was for this reason that the tree had withered up and become all hollow. And now down on the body there fell also the bag of pearls. Hardly could he be at rest; that most restless man!

Now let us turn to the girl. When she woke up she saw that there was no one there with her, neither the boy nor the muleteers. She washed her face in the cold water and began to put her hair tidy. Then she saw that the little bag was not there. She began to cry, but what she could do she did not know. She stayed there some time longer. Then she became afraid of being there all by herself, and took out of the luggage a suit of boy's clothes. She put them on and turned herself into a young man. She left all the things there and went off by the nearest path. In trying to follow the boy, she went back again to her father's city. Then in the evening the muleteers came back to the spring; they found that there was no one anywhere there. They waited until it got dark; no one was to be seen. They waited there, and in the morning, since no one came, they shared out the goods and went off to their houses.

The girl in her boy's clothes turned back again to the city looking to find the boy. No one could give her any clear answer and she could never find out anything. She pondered much over the matter, but never had she any suspicion at all that the boy might perhaps have taken the pearls and gone off with them. Several times she went to her father's fine house: it was always locked up; her father and her mother were still away searching for her: who could be sure that they were not dead from grief? She made up her mind to stop in the city and there to await the coming of the boy. At the landing-place in the harbour there was a grubby, dirty man who had a tavern; but he was so uncleanly that no one ever set his foot in the place. To him went the young lad—for from now we shall call the girl so—and asked for work. 'Master,' said she, 'let me come and be with you as your servant: I will work for you and you shall give me some wages.' 'No one ever sets his foot in here; from the trade I have I can't live myself, and what can I have to give you?' 'I will look after your tavern and it will do very well; then you can pay me so that I too can have a living.' So answered the boy. 'Very well,' said the man of the tavern. 'Come here and stay with me and we will see how things turn out.'

At this the boy was very well pleased: she would be all the time down at the landing-place, seeing all comers and everyone going to foreign parts, and perhaps she might come across the boy, the Son of Wealth. So with delight she rolled up her sleeves and tied on an apron and set to work. She swept the room and washed it and kept everything clean: the tavern was quite a new place. If a man once came and took coffee there, he never left the place afterwards. It got a good name and patrons multiplied. By now the girl was not sufficient for all the work and they took on a young boy. Within a year they had made a great deal of money, and by the side of the tavern they built some fine rooms for guests: these were called 'the boys' rooms'. All those who were on their way to or coming from foreign lands used to go and stop there. The keeper of the tavern was very fond of his young lad and it came to his mind to marry him to his daughter. He told him this and the boy was willing; they agreed that after three years they would make the marriage. The boy was the owner's right hand and by his zealous service they made any amount of money.

The three years passed by. All this time the boy had been working hard tending his vine, and it had produced fine grapes. He took some good bunches and brought them to the ruler of the city. Much pleased, the ruler gave the boy leave to go to his own country and the right to take with him whatever things he chose. The boy was delighted and began to make his preparations. As soon as he had everything ready, he went in the evening to cut some grapes from his vine, to have them with him on his way. When he came near he stood still in astonishment; the three withered poplars at the edge of the vineyard had been blown down by the wind and had fallen on the vine and broken it; no grapes were to be found. Then as he walked by the roots of the poplar trees, something caught his eye. He went closer and what did he see? Underneath the root of each of the trees there was a small jar filled with gold coins, and lying on the top of the central jar was the little bag with the jewels and pearls. He was so delighted as to be quite in a daze: what was he to do? At once he hid the little bag away in his pocket and conveyed the three jars to his room. He took the gold coins out of the jars and packed them up in the rest of his luggage. In the morning he took his things, embarked on the ship, and went off. In a day and a night he had reached the girl's city. He landed at the harbour and was thinking where he should go to lodge, when the servant of the tavern man came up and took him off to 'the boys' rooms'. The young man—don't forget that this is the girl—recognized the newcomer and told the serving-boy to put him into the best room. The boy looked at this young man and said to himself: 'This boy seems to me like someone; he looks like a girl, and very much like the girl who was with me; but then, if it is a girl, why should she be wearing boy's clothes?' He looked at her once more and once again, and then went to his room. He rested a while and then fell asleep; he was tired and had suffered very much from the sea.

In the evening the girl went round all the rooms and looked into what the strangers had to pay. The last one she went to was the room of the boy, the Son of Wealth. She went in to say 'Good evening' to him, and then, instead of looking into his bill, she questioned him: 'Where have you come from, my good lad? And what is your country?' 'Don't ask me from what country I come; it distresses me; look into my bill,' said the boy. 'You must tell me who you are and from what country and what are your troubles,' said the girl again, and pressed him to tell her. The boy no longer made any resistance and poured it all out; he told her to the last detail everything that he had gone through. His throat choked and his eyes swam with tears. 'And you,' said he, 'are very like my little sister, and if you were a girl I should have said you were she;' and his tears fell like hail. The girl could endure this no longer. She uncovered her hair and it poured down over her shoulders. 'It is I,' she said, and fell into the boy's arms. They embraced one another, and kissed and cried; in their happiness they fainted away. Then they came to again, and when they had recovered their senses and quieted down, the girl too told him all her afflictions. Presently they arranged their plan for running away and the girl rolled up her hair and covered it and went back to the tavern.

Next day in the morning she asked the keeper of the tavern for leave to be absent, saying to him: 'The stranger who was in the best room is from our village and he is now on his way there. When my parents hear this they will ask questions and find out that I am here and be vexed and say: "Why didn't he come with the stranger?" Also it is now three years that I have not seen my parents, and I have been longing for them. Let me go to the village with him. Nor will I ever find a better companion than him. Give me leave to go and see my parents and take their blessing. Perhaps I can persuade them to come here and they too be present at my wedding.' The man was quite content with this and had nothing to say. He gave her leave to go and stay for a while with her father and her mother, for of course he and they were parents of a boy and girl to be married. And he also sent them presents.

Dressed as a boy the girl took a little pocket-money for the journey, and the stranger went and bought two changes of women's clothes. When they had made everything ready they took muleteers and started for their village. When they were some way from the city the girl took off her boy's clothes and put on the clothes which the boy had bought for her: so dressed she looked a fine girl.

Then again they resolved to go up to the Pastures of the

Sun. There they made their way upwards to the ridge and came out to the top of it. There they turned and came down to the same little spring where the girl had fallen asleep and the bird had carried off the pearls. This time they did not remain there but just stayed for a little to rest and drink water. By the side of the spring there was stirring in the breeze a little flower like those which had served to guide her to follow when the boy had gone away. She plucked a twig with three flowers on it and twisted it up in a corner of her kerchief to keep it as a treasure. Then they followed down a little valley and passed through meadows and vales and hollow places, and in five days they came to the Pastures of the Sun. There in a fine and lofty place they built their house. The girl gave him the plan on which it should be built: it was like her father's big house. Everyone heard that on the Pastures of the Sun a stranger had built a marvellous dwelling. By means of news from one place and another the boy found out what his father and his mother were doing, but he never let himself be seen by them. His father and his mother spent much money in searching for him but they could find him nowhere. They wept and were much grieved. His poor mother wept so much that she lost the sight of her eyes and became blind. Night and day she wept and uttered lamentations for her son, and so with Alas! and Woe is me! she passed her days.

Now let us go and look at the father and the mother of the girl: we told you that they went out to look for her, and for three years they were seeking for her. They went to all the three cantons of the world and could not find her. From her sorrow and from her much weeping her mother's eyes had clouded and she could not see. The ship's captain led her by the hand and so they went their way. It happened that they were passing over the ridge of the mountain where the boy, the Son of Wealth, and the girl had passed when they had stayed there by the spring and their daughter had fallen asleep. As they were sitting there a strange bird, like the one which had belonged to the moneychanger, came and perched by the water. The bird drank a little and began to sing, and what it sang was this: 'If you knew my language your trouble would be at an end. Take this flower and open your eyes. Follow me and you will attain your desires.' The wife of the rich man understood the languages of birds. She understood what the bird said and told her husband. At once he picked the flower and gave it to her into her hand. She rubbed it on her eyes and they were made well; she saw better than she had seen before. They were full of delight and rose up and went following the bird. The bird in front and they following behind, in four days they came up on the Pastures of the Sun. The bird went off and the two of them began searching this way and that to find their daughter. In the distance they saw a building and the captain said: 'That house looks very like our own fine dwelling; Let us go there and ask; it may be that the people there know something about our daughter.' They went straight there. Looking at the house they were astonished: it was exactly like their own palace; no difference at all! They came up as far as the outer gateway and begged the porter to ask the master of the house whether he would receive strangers. The girl from inside heard this and came to the window to see what strangers these were. When she looked, lo, at the outside gate she saw standing her own father and mother. She ran off and told the boy: she herself remained hidden. The boy received the strangers and brought them into the house. Before they were well seated, the captain said: 'If it be possible, my lad, I beg you to tell me who it was laid down the plan of your house; it is like our own house in the city.' 'The plan of this house of mine was laid down by a girl who was of your city,' said the boy. The man and his wife looked at one another and the woman asked: 'And where is the girl now?' 'She is here,' said the boy. 'She is asleep, but let me go and wake her up and bring her here.' He opened the door, and there was the girl standing before them; she ran forward and fell into their arms. They embraced her and kissed her; with their joy all of them burst into tears.

The girl sat down and told them everything that had befallen her: how she had escaped and how it was that she was there. They also told what they had seen and what had happened to them in the three years when they were searching for her. The boy, too, told them the story of his troubles. When they had stayed there quietly for some days, the boy said to the girl: 'We have found your father and your mother, now let us go off and find mine, my father and my mother.'

They went off to the boy's village. His father had grown old from grief and his mother too was in her bed laid up. So they came and found them there and the old people were so happy that what to do they knew not. The father from his joy you might have thought a young man again; but for his mother one would have been sorry because she had no eyes to look at her darling. 'Oh, if only we had that flower which we found by the spring up there on the mountain!' said the girl's father, the captain. 'With that flower I cured my eyes,' said her mother. The girl asked what kind of flower that was. Then she danced for joy and said: 'I have one of those very flowers.' She had it knotted up in a corner of her kerchief. They rubbed it on the old woman's eyes and she was cured. Their joy reached even as high as heaven. Each of them knew everything of the others and all their life was of honey and milk. After some while they held the wedding of their son and sent invitations to all the villages. They celebrated the wedding for forty days and forty nights, and they all lived happily and we in yet greater happiness.

And the poor man who kept the tavern is still waiting for the young chap.

24

The two Pauls

THIS Pontic story is simply a novel, and like most of these novels is recorded from only one place, where it presumably originated, and not so very long ago. Typologically these novels come at the end of the folktale series, and equally late is another point: we have in this story at least the beginning of a feeling for character. The simple contrast between a good man and a bad man is common enough in these stories, and inevitable, but here we have a little more, and the main interest lies in the contrast between the simple and honest country chap and his cunning and rascally 'opposite number', Paul of the City, with the ultimate triumph of Paul of the Village. Most primitive tales are based on a situation which must be developed towards a happy ending. In the present story we have exactly the opposite: the narrative is arranged to exhibit the contrast between the two central actors, almost like a modern novel, in which character is vastly more important than situation. In one of his essays R. L. Stevenson drew the distinction between the novels based on a situation and those based on the characters of the people concerned. The typical folktale belongs to the former class; *The two Pauls* moves very distinctly towards the latter.

The notion that all created things are made in pairs is found in other stories, and I have said about it all that is needful in *M.G.F.*, p. 376, where I have quoted from the recently translated Persian book of the eleventh century, *The Mirror of Princes*,[1] in which it is brought into connexion with the much stressed Islamic doctrine of the unity of God: all created things partake in some way of the notion of 'Twoness', of duality; God alone is the One.

The feeling that there exists between father and son a special corporal connexion is, in this story, illustrated by the episode of the son's blood cleaving to the father's bone. It is found again in No. 6 above, where the paste kneaded from the ashes of the father's body can be eaten by the son, but will be instantly fatal to anyone else, as dangerous as in modern medical practice the use of a wrong type of blood for a transfusion.

[1] *Mirror of Princes*. Translated by Reuben Levy, 1951, p. 8.

NO. 24. THE TWO PAULS[1]

Once upon a time, the tale began,
When the Turks were keeping Ramazan.

There was in a village of Katephoria a widow, and she had a son. When he was very young she got him a wife, and this young woman was big and strong and well able to work, and in this way they could all have a living. The marriage was fine and fair, and they all started working. But whatever they undertook, their work never prospered, and they were so poor that they could hardly keep their eyes from shutting. Before this they had been poor, but now things were still worse. The youth tried hard, but to no purpose, and was indeed in very evil plight. Then it came to his mind to do as his neighbours did and go to some foreign land, and in this way he might find work and make some money. He arranged for the expenses of the journey and set out. His mother and his wife saw him off, and when they were taking leave, he took his mother aside and said to her in private: 'Mother—and so may I see you once more—take good care of my wife.' Then he kissed them and went off. He walked for ten hours and then he came to the town. Next day he went on board the steamer, and so to a foreign land. In the place where he had come he knew no one, but his good luck came to his aid and after two days he found a good place and started to work. He worked hard, but there was nothing to be made by it; he worked and he worked but scarcely could he make his expenses. He turned this way and he turned that way; he pressed himself; even to exhaustion; all to no purpose; he could not get any money above the needful. Years came and years went, and he never could send anything home. Poor Paul, the Son of Ill Luck! for so indeed they called him. He was all but losing his wits; what he could do he did not know.

One day when he was sitting miserably in the tavern, he heard some people talking about jobs of work. He listened and heard that in another town they were building roads and bridges, and starting on a great deal of work. Without asking

[1] Text from Stavrín in Pontos, printed in *Arkheion Pontou*, xii. 176.

any questions to make sure, he left the tavern and went to his room. There he set his things in order and the next day he boarded the steamer and went to this other town. He disembarked, set his pack on his back, and went to the strangers' tavern; he sat down at a table and ordered a tea. As he was drinking his tea, he saw that all those round him were staring at him. This staring he did not like, but he said nothing. He heard them whispering: 'He's very like Paul of the City.' 'Just such another: he's exactly like him.' 'Shut up; this is another chap.' All this he could not understand: what he was thinking of was to find some job. 'What is your name, my lad?' a fellow asked him. 'Paul they call me, my uncle.' 'That's Paul all right,' whispered another, standing a little apart. 'He is out to play some trick on us.' One of the men who had been sitting in the tavern went out into the market, and there he saw Paul of the City, and he asked him: 'As you love God; just now I came out of the tavern and left you there: you can't have had time to get here to the market before me.' 'What are you talking about? I have only just now come out of my house, and haven't been to the tavern at all,' said Paul of the City. 'Come, come, my friend; I saw you in the tavern a moment ago, and now you tell me you have not been away from your house.' So the fellow said and went off angrily.

Paul of the City, a regular devil, saw that there was something up, and very quickly he found his way to the tavern. He went in and what did he see? Inside there was sitting a young fellow just like himself: split an apple, and with the halves you would have had the two of them. 'They say well,' said he to himself, 'that in the world all men have their double,' and he went up close to the village fellow. He greeted him and began asking him one thing and another: where he was from; what work he did; and how he had chanced to come to the town. Paul, the Man of Ill Luck, especially as he was a little simple, gave him an account of his troubles and of his condition. Paul of the City was very encouraging and said: 'Well, my namesake, do not be troubled. I have work on hand and have need of craftsmen and workmen; you come and work with me.' Then he took him off to his house. Three days passed and they got to know one another very well, working together like this. They took up a contract and set to work. They engaged many workmen and their business grew. The two Pauls, friends and fellow craftsmen, ate both of them together, drank together, and together went to their work; their purse also was in common. Men looked at them with admiration, but all the time they said to themselves: 'For success look to the end: March comes in and what the month will be like no one knows; it is at the end that men will judge what it has been.'

As they were working together that rascal Paul of the City carefully watched the village fellow's manner of life: how he talked; how he joked; all this he impressed on his memory. He questioned him about his house, about his mother, about his wife, about his kinsmen and his neighbours; about his fields and his gardens and all that he had. He learned all this to the last detail; better than the man knew it himself. All that he could not keep in his head he wrote down in his notebook so as not to forget it.

So in this way they worked for a long time, and when they had finished a certain piece of their work, Paul of the City went to the royal treasury to draw money and come and pay the workmen and the craftsmen. Then, with the money in his pocket, a couple of hundred nice red gold pieces, he disappeared; where he had gone no one knew. On that day a steamer had come on her way to Katephoria; Paul had embarked on her and gone off. Two days later he left the steamer at the village fellow's town. He went to the inn and found a muleteer, a man who came from his village, and they got acquainted. Then Paul hired his horses; he loaded them with spirits, cognac, sugar, coffee, cloth, coloured stuffs, and many other things: then they started off for the village. On the way he questioned the muleteer and found out whatever he did not yet know. In the evening they arrived at the village and came to the country fellow's house. When they were near someone saw them and ran and announced their coming to the widow and to Paul's wife.

'May light shine on your eyes, Auntie! Your son has come. Light on your eyes, wife! Your husband has come!' 'And may your eyes be full of light!' cried the women and ran to meet the man. They embraced him and kissed him and went off to the house. All the village heard of the coming of Paul the Unlucky, and all those who had been children with him ran up to see him. His kinsmen and neighbours all came in crowds. They made him welcome and sat down talking. Some of them he could not recognize and his mother told him who they were. 'And is it a short time he has been away in foreign lands?' His wife too was saying: 'Fine that he remembers it all so well.' The visiting came to an end, and when his kinsmen and their visitors were about to go away, Paul, with the consent of his mother, gave each of them a present. When he had dismissed them all, he opened his luggage and showed his old mother and his wife the good and fine things which he had brought and all the gold pieces which he had in his belt. 'Mother,' said he, 'all your debts and all your little owings you must tell me and I will pay them all. I don't want to have anything here belonging rightly to any other man. And of all these things here take and wear whatever your heart desires.' The old woman and his wife were beside themselves: so much delighted that what to do they knew not. They washed his head; they washed his feet; they gave him a change of clothes, and then they went off to bed.

Next day his wife rose up in the morning jumping for joy, and by the time her mother-in-law and her husband were awake she had done all the work of the house. When they also had got up and had had a meal, Paul said to the mother: 'Mother, let us go to the house of my uncle the Pilgrim. He is in mourning and that is why he did not come when the people were welcoming me.' 'Very well,' said the mother; 'let us go.' And so they made ready. They took half a sugar-loaf, a tin of coffee, and a nice little lot of tobacco, and went to the Pilgrim's house. A modest young married woman when she saw that the old mother and Paul had gone to the Pilgrim's house, ran off to Paul's house. She found his wife all full of joy and questioned her about her husband who had been abroad. 'If you only knew what a fine fellow he is,' said Paul's wife. 'When he went abroad he was rather out of health, but now you can see that he is as fine as an angel; so may I rejoice in his life!' 'And may joy be yours,' said the modest young woman, and went off.

An hour later Paul and his mother came back. The meal was ready and they sat down and ate and after midday they went again to visit other kinsmen. Next day they went and saw others, and so they made the rounds and saw all their kinsfolk and all their neighbours, and to all they brought some little present. On Sunday Paul had a Mass said for his father, and mention was made in it of all their dead. Then after church they invited everyone to come to their house and there they ate and drank. Also to the priest he gave a double fee. All the world very clearly recognized Paul and all gave him their love and respect. He seemed to work magic and never did he offend anyone. He made all the people in the village his friends and so he lived there a very pleasant life.

Now let us leave Paul of the City in all this happiness and pass to see what was happening to Paul the Villager there in the foreign land. The unlucky fellow was there waiting and waiting for his companion to come with the money, and when his patience was at an end he got up and ran to the treasury and asked about his friend. He was told that the man had made his reckoning, taking two hundred pieces, good red gold, and had signed the quittance. Paul the Villager went off like a madman. Workmen and craftsmen swarmed round his head demanding their day-by-day money. Paul was so much troubled that he flew into a rage with them and cried: 'Don't shout and scream, you fellows; the man was not of that sort. Who can say what has happened to him? It may be that when he was bringing the money robbers attacked him and killed him and carried off the money. Do not be afraid; your wages shan't be lost; I will set to work and pay you.' Thus the workmen were for a little time quiet. The foreman heard what had happened and was much grieved. He was sorry for Paul and went and comforted him. 'Don't be afraid,' he said. 'I am here and as long as I can I will keep hold of your hand.' Also he said to the workmen and to the craftsmen: 'You go on working until the job is finished, and for all your money you can come upon me.'

The village fellow started to work with a good heart, night and day, never stopping. In two months he had brought all the work to an end. He paid the workmen and the craftsmen and with what was left to him he cleared just a poor hundred pence. Then he began to get ready to go to his own country. He had a little pleasant rest and quiet with his friends and with the foreman; this was a great delight to them all. Next day he said 'Farewell' to all of them and went on board the steamer. On the voyage he was thinking: 'And what indeed can ever have happened to my companion Paul? If he has played me', for so he was saying to himself, 'some devilish trick with the money, then joy may he never see, and may God come down from heaven and do justice upon him. Yet if robbers have killed him and taken the money, then may God give him his pardon: he was a good fellow. There is no other way: I must seek and search and find out what has happened.' As all this was in his mind, he fell into a long sleep.

When he woke up he saw that the steamer was in the harbour of his own town. He rose up well pleased, and with all that he had he disembarked and went to the inn. He bought one thing and another for his mother and his wife; he got some provisions for his house and made everything ready for his return home. Next day he hired a horse and loaded up his things and went off on the way to his village. No one recognized him and he did not tell the muleteer who he was. It was not yet quite dark when he came to the village. He went straight to his house and knocked at the door. 'Who are you?' asked his mother from inside. 'Open, mother; it's me.' 'And who are you?' said the old woman again. 'Mother, I am your son Paul; open the door.' 'You go right away from here. My son Paul is here in the house.' 'What are you saying, mother? Are you mad? What son of yours can be here?' 'You go right away: I don't know you and I won't open the door.'

When Paul of the City heard their dispute, the fleas as it were began to bite him. 'Mother, see you don't open the door. Drive them away; it looks as if they were robbers. They have found out that we have some money and they have come to rob us. See you don't open the door.' Paul of the Village cried and shouted, but nothing happened: they would not open the door. 'A damned odd way you're behaving. This is a very strange affair. Well, we must see how it will all turn out.' So they went and untied the baggage at the door of the stable and stayed there outside, but no sleep came to their eyes. In the morning Paul called for the headman and the members of the council and the neighbours and told them his position; he told them all that had happened. But nothing was to be done; they all assured him that Paul of the City was the son of the old woman and that he was telling lies. 'Who knows what troublesome fellow this is? His mother and his wife would not accept him.' The modest young woman had something she wanted to say, but her mother-in-law began to scold her.

Paul of the Village became like one mad; what to do he knew not. Then a kindly man took him into his house and advised him to go to the law court and report this business of his. The case lasted a long time. The Twelve Councillors questioned the villagers and questioned the two Pauls, but they could not make out which of them was in the right. Many traps they set to catch them, but the boys fell into none of them. What the village boy, and he was a man of God, said was always the truth; yet the boy from the city, a clever devil, was never caught out. The Twelve Councillors thought over the matter and thought over it again, but could come to no decision.

Then from some place or other a dervish came to them; he too had had some business with the court. When he heard of the difficulty in which the Twelve found themselves, he laughed: 'But isn't this an easy matter?' said he. 'I can find out which of the two Pauls is the son of the old woman.' With this the Twelve were content, and gave him leave to do what he could. Losing no time, the dervish took the two Pauls and with the Councillors went to the village. He set them to open the tomb of the father, and each of the Pauls took a fragment of the bones of his hand. The bones were washed and well dried. Then said the dervish to Paul of the City: 'Cut your finger and let a little blood drop on the bone.' At once the man cut his finger and did as the dervish told him.

They let the blood dry on the bone and then wiped it with a cloth: all the blood was wiped right away and on the bone not a trace of it remained. The dervish told Paul of the Village to do the same, and he too did as the dervish told him. When the blood of the village boy had dried on the bone, they tried to wipe it off and clear it away, but it had hardened on the bone and no rubbing could take it away. Everyone was astonished; the Councillors were stricken stiff. 'This second man,' said the dervish, 'is the man's son; he is the son of the old woman and the husband of the girl.' So the Twelve gave their decision in favour of Paul of the Village, and to the dervish they said: 'What you have done is a thing far beyond our comprehension. Now go your ways and prosper.' So the dervish went away.

Paul of the City was given for his supper seven loads of stick, and off he ran and he is still running. Paul of the Village went to his house. He had a fine Mass celebrated for his father. With both his mother and his wife he was reconciled, but he never came near them or had any dealings with them. After no long time his mother died of her disgrace. His wife too was so much shamed that she drowned herself in the river. So Paul was left alone by himself. People no longer spoke of Paul the Son of Ill Luck, but they called him Paul the Wealthy. Everyone in the village respected him.

At that time in another village there was a great festival. The villagers with some other villagers fell to disputing about nothing at all: it was a very grievous affair. Knives were drawn, guns were brought out, and many men were wounded. The husband of the modest young wife was struck by a bullet and after three days died. All lamented for him, and for the good of his soul Paul spent lavishly. The young bride who had so sadly become a widow, and with no children, went off to her parents' house. After a year Paul the Wealthy wished to marry, and he took as his wife the modest young bride. Happily did they all live and may we live in still greater happiness.

25

The Next World

THIS account of the Next World, of the souls of the blessed and of the wicked dead, and how they can be helped by the pious deeds of the living, recorded more than fifty years ago in Chios by Kanellakis, has been cast into the form of a folktale. The three brothers in search of their sister, who just as she was to be married was carried off by the whirlwind of death, is in the true folktale style; so too is their leaving their rings at the point where the road divides. In orthodox belief it is Michael the Archangel who carries off the souls of the dying; here he is not mentioned, and the guide to the Next World is, to me quite unexpectedly, St. George. Nor is Kharos mentioned; this descendant of the ancient Charon, who in popular ballads carries off the souls of the dying, belongs to a way of looking at death much more pagan than in any way of the Orthodox Church.

It is an interesting point that the happy souls are found keeping Easter. One of the most poignant things in the popular Greek laments for the dead is that they are by death cut off from the social pleasures of the living, and of these one of the greatest is Easter; the dead are particularly missed when all the living embrace one another for joy in the Resurrection. I may quote from a lament from Karpathos recorded by Mikhaïlídis-Nouáros in his *Laographiká sýmmeikta Karpáthou*, i. 130. It is sung on Good Friday and the mourner asks the dead man: 'Tell me, in the black, the black cobwebby earth, do the dead indeed deck the bier of Christ? Do they indeed keep Easter and bake the round buns for the feast? Do they bring flowers to celebrate the Resurrection?'

It is not here the place to go into the literature of visions of the Next World, but two popular Greek texts ought to be mentioned as of exactly the same kind as this present story. The first is from Thrace, printed in *Thrakiká*, ii. 146. It is a very brief piece taken down from a woman. It tells how on Saturday in Holy Week the Virgin went in a chariot drawn by three hundred angels to visit the souls of the condemned. The latter part is in verse, using much of the material to be found in the popular laments for the dead. How far the prose part—half a page only—is allied to any written account I do not know. As in our piece, one of the sinners is a woman who had given suck to a Turkish baby.

This same sin is mentioned in the second piece I adduce. This is in a manuscript preserved in the Marcian Library at Venice; it is in Cretan Greek but in Latin characters, and so presumably belongs to the latter part of the Venetian period in Crete, when the island had attained a certain degree of prosperity. It belongs to a whole series of *Apokalypseis* of the Virgin, in which oral and literary sources are clearly mixed together. Again we have the pretty touch that the souls of children are diverted from any longing for their mothers by the sound of bells played by the angels for their amusement. The text is partly printed with commentary in *Byzantinische Zeitschrift*, xxx. 300, and in full, but transcribed into Greek characters, in *Kritiká Khroniká*, ii. 487.

NO. 25. THE NEXT WORLD[1]

A king had three sons, and after some time a daughter also was born. At her birth his wife had died, so the king took a nurse for the girl, and when she became a little bigger he took also a woman to give her her lessons. She never knew any other human being except only the nurse and the teacher.

Some years after she was born the king also died and so the sons and the girl were left orphans. The sons therefore began to consider about their sister, that it was their duty to arrange a good marriage for her. Their idea was to display her one day on her couch and proclaim that all the young knights in turn should pass by on their horses, as is the wont of the sons of emperors and of kings, and whichever of them was pleasing to her, him they should give her for her husband. And as they had resolved, so it was done. The parade began; one by one, all chosen youths, armed with their swords, their lances, and their bows. Then the girl asked what things were these passing by in front of her. And while the whole affair was being explained to her, there came a great whirlwind which carried everything away with it: the dust was so thick that no man could see his fellow. When this terrible wind was over, the brothers saw that the girl was no longer on the couch. They sought and searched for her in this place and

[1] Unpublished text from Chios, recorded by Kanellakis.

in that, but they could not find her; so they sent out men and hunters and hounds to seek for her, in every cleft in the ground and in every well, in the valleys and on the hills, and wherever else they thought they might find her, but they could not find her anywhere. When the men sent out for this purpose could not find her, the brothers themselves determined to go off as best they might to look for her.

So they went along a road, and as they were going on all of them together, they came to a place where the road divided into three, and in the midst of the place where the roads parted there was a big slab, and on it was written that two of the roads led to towns and places from which if a man wished he could return, but the third road admitted of no return; whoever went that way would never come back again. The three brothers therefore cast lots to see on whom would fall the lot to go on the road with no return, and the lot fell on the youngest brother. Yet since it was indeed hard to make up their minds on such a question, who should go on a road which allowed no return, they took the lots yet twice more, and for the second and again for the third time the lot fell on the youngest brother.

So when they saw this strange happening, the youngest one said that they should place their rings underneath the stone with the writing, and each one on returning should take his own ring, and so they would know who had come back.

So each of them went on the road which had been determined, and the youngest went on and on, and he saw no man at all, neither city nor village; then after many days he saw a man and called out to him. But the man said nothing in answer. When he came up close to him, the youth began to speak in his ear because he thought he was deaf. And when he came close up to him, the man fell down, and the poor prince thought that he had broken his bones or was dead, and he began to think what he should do. Thinking of this he walked on, always going farther, and close by the road he saw a palace; he went into it to see what there was inside. And he saw that the people there were all young girls dancing and singing, dances and songs of holy maidenhood. And when they saw him, they hushed, and ceased dancing. When he went up close to them, at once they fell to the ground. And when he saw things were thus, he went away from that palace and went on still farther. Then as he was on his way he came to a lofty castle, and its windows and its door were of iron, and he saw that it would be hard to open them and go into the castle. As he was thinking what he should do, his horse neighed, and at once his sister reached out from the window above, for she had recognized the voice of his horse, and seeing her brother she cried out. When he saw her there, no lobster in the sea could have been deafer, more remote from comprehension, than he was, for he had never thought that he would meet her in that place. And when he came to his senses, he asked her how she came to be there. Then he told her how all the three of them had set out to look for her, and how each one had gone on his own way. Then again he asked her how she came to be there, and she told him the story, how at the moment of the whirlwind a youth with a lance in his hand and girt with a sword had come and carried her off and set her on his horse and brought her to that castle, and how when she had come to herself she had asked him who he was, and he had told her that he was St. George, and how from that day she had been there, always in very great happiness.

When she had finished her story she told him to stay there until St. George came back, and he would open the door for him to come up into the castle, because she could not open it. And after a few minutes St. George came and opened the gate which was of iron, and brought the prince up. And when he had stayed there two or three days he had had enough and wanted to go and visit all those regions. The saint told him to take his own horse—the horse knew the way—and ride round. He told him not to speak, and when people spoke to him he must hold his tongue as though he were dumb, and when he saw any need he must pull at the horse's bridle, and so go on farther.

The prince sat on the saint's horse, and as he was going his way he saw a garden: it was all planted with scented violets. Those who were in that garden were all little children, holding hands with one another and singing and dancing.

And when they saw him they told him to dismount and dance because they were celebrating Easter. But the youth continued riding about the garden; then he went away. And as he was going on his way, he came to another pleasaunce, and it was full of beautiful rose-trees, and those who were there were all young girls, singing and dancing. And when they saw him they told him to come and dance because they were keeping Easter. But the young man continued riding about the garden. Then he pulled at the bridle and went farther. And on the way he came upon yet another garden all full of the very reddest carnations, and those in it were all young men; they too were dancing. And when they saw him they also told him to come and dance because they were keeping Easter. But when he had ridden about among them to his fill he pulled at the bridle of the horse and moved farther on. Then on his way he saw a tree all of gold and it was thronged with birds and with young angels, and if the birds began to complain, then the angels rang the bells which they had in their hands in order that the little birds might no more remember their mothers.

When the youth had fully seen all this, he went on his way. And as he was going he saw a tree which seemed all covered in black; on it was a flock of crows beyond all counting, all crying out 'Kra, kra'. And as they cried at that moment a red fire issued from their mouths.

Then he left that place and came to a field; it was full of women. Some were set on fiery spikes; others had snakes going in at one ear and coming out at the other. And when he had beheld them he went away. And going farther on, suddenly he saw a river which was all of fire, and in it there were wineskins, some going up the river and some going down. Departing thence on his way he came up to a great church; all the men in it were priests. Some were hanged up by their tongues and some by the head and others by the feet. Others too had only their heads inside the door of the church and their bodies were outside. And when he had looked at those inside the church, he departed from that place.

And as he was on his way he came to a marsh, and in it were many pigs, and at two of the pigs in it he looked with great curiosity because one was going and biting the other and the second pig was biting the first, and they continued this biting without intermission. And for these two pigs he was heartily sorry, weeping to see their pitiable case.

When he had finished looking at all the things which we have told of—and there were many other things which a man would find it grievous to recount; they would drive him out of his mind—he turned and went to the castle. St. George asked him what he had seen on his journey, and he began to tell him all the story. And St. George expounded to him that those violets are the little children who had not yet known the meaning of sin; the rose-trees are young maidens; the carnations are youths of innocent life. The birds on the golden tree were all little babies not yet knowing even their alpha and omega, and the angels play to them on little bells to prevent them from crying when they remember their mothers. The black tree shows men who were sinners, and the women sitting on stools were all of them sinners; and those giving suck to puppies were those who gave suck to children of strange religions, and those with snakes coming in at their ears were those who sit close to listen to everybody's family secrets. The wineskins which were floating up and down on the fiery river, these were of the nation of the Jews. As for the church, those hanged up by the tongue are those who wasted the rich jewels of the church; and those who were hanged by the hand were those who wasted the money of the church, and the same for those who were hanging by the feet. Those whose bodies were outside the church and their heads inside were sinful priests. The pigs in the marsh were sinful kings, 'and those who were biting one another were your mother and your father, and their biting one another signifies that one of them is speaking to the other, and she never allowed him either to do good to the people of his realm or perform any works of mercy.' At all this the prince was much grieved, but for his parents he was indeed sorrowful at heart. So he rose up and departed.

And when he had come to the place of the three roads where the slab was with their rings hidden underneath it, he lifted it up and found only his own ring, so he understood that his brothers had come back, and he went his way and came himself to the palace and found his brothers. He told them that they need have no care about their sister because she was very well indeed where he had found her, and that she could find no better place. Then he asked them to make a division of their substance, because he wanted to take his share and go whithersoever the light of God should lead him. So he took the share that was due to him and divided it among the poor in order that he might be able to set his parents free. When he had distributed it, he mounted his horse and went to St. George. Then on his way he came upon a palace which he had not seen the first time he went that way; he went up to have a look at the palace but in it he found no one at all.

Now when he came to the castle he asked for the saint's horse that he might go and see his parents, if they had received any benefit from the act of charity which he had done for their sakes. And when he came to the marsh he again found them in the same plight, and full of sorrow he came back to the castle. Then St. George told him that the palace which he had seen by the way had been built for him because of the gifts which he had distributed in charity, and that if his parents had done acts of mercy and kindness to their people, they too would have been saved and sanctified.

When the youth heard all that St. George said to him, he asked him how he could save them, and the saint showed him a mountain and told him to go there to find a virtuous ascetic. So he went, and the ascetic was amazed to see him, for never in the place where he was leading the ascetic life did any man come, and here was this youth begging that he might dwell with him. The ascetic answered that he should wait till the next day to have his answer.

In front of his cave the ascetic had a pomegranate tree and every morning on his tree he found a pomegranate and a small loaf; on that morning he had found two pomegranates and two loaves, and he understood that it was the will of God that the prince should remain with him. So the prince passed a whole year there, and at the end of the year, by the consent of the ascetic, he went to see about his parents. And when he came to the castle he mounted on St. George's horse and went to the marsh, and he saw his parents abiding there fully at peace, no longer biting one another, and he understood that they had had some small benefit. And thus he returned to the castle, and the saint told him to go and live the ascetic life for yet another year.

He did as the saint had bidden him and at the end of the full year he came back and went to the marsh. He could not find his father and mother there, and did not know what to think and suppose. So to be at rest he went and told the saint, and the saint assured him that their sins were done away and that they would not be punished in hell any more. When the youth heard this his soul was thankful and he was utterly filled with joy. Also he abode in the palace built for him because of his charitable acts, done by the command of Him who judges the good and the evil deeds of men.

26

The Man who would avoid Death

THIS kind of optimistic submission to what is in the course of nature is a part of the Greek philosophy of life, which has always been to live 'in accordance with nature', *κατὰ τὴν φύσιν*. I do not know this present story from Pontos elsewhere, but there are several stories in which we see death kept away by some ingenious device, and then at last welcomed as a deliverer, if not from life, yet from the troubles and tedium of old age.

Of this I find a more than half humorous example in a story from Thrace, printed in *Thrakiká*, xvii. 172. It is of an old woman, as they are commonly seen in Greek folktales: crafty, generally kindly, infinitely resourceful, indulgently laughed at, yet always admired. Here is the story in outline.

An old woman had a pear-tree and was much troubled because boys used to climb it and steal the pears. She appealed to St. Polycarp—whose name, 'Of much Fruit', makes him a suitable guardian for fruit trees—and the saint gave the very doubtful blessing to the tree that whoever climbed up it would stick among the branches; this checked the boys. In due time Kharos—the Charon of ancient Greece, but now in modern ideas the minister and messenger of death—came to fetch the old woman. Before starting on her long journey, the old woman had the happy idea of persuading him to climb the tree and pick a few pears to eat on the way. Death, like the boys, found himself stuck among the branches, and could not come down, and the old woman escaped death. But there was now no one to carry away the souls of the old people ready for death, and the village doctor was in despair with so many elderly Struldbrugs on his hands. He found where Death was, but that was no remedy. At last the old woman grew so very old that she longed to be relieved of the burden of life. Supported by her staff, she hobbled to the tree, she alone being able to bring Death down to the ground. Then Death was free to lead away all the souls ready for the Next World, and among them, of course, the soul of the old woman.

In Bolte and Polivka, *Anmerkungen*, ii. 163, 189, we have a great deal of material about the binding of Death and his being prevented from performing his natural function, and we even read, on p. 172, of Death up in a pear-tree, from which he cannot come down: this is in a book of sermons printed in 1700. The idea of Death bound goes back to classical times.

NO. 26. THE MAN WHO WOULD AVOID DEATH[1]

There was once a man who was so very much afraid of death that when it was even mentioned in his presence he used to run away and hide himself. At last he had the idea to search over all the world, and he would go and live in whatever place Death was never mentioned and there were no tombs. So he wandered over many lands and at last he came to a place where he observed that men never spoke of death, nor in that land were there any tombs. He asked a man why there were no tombs to be seen. 'In this place', said the man, 'we know nothing of death, nor of what tombs may be, only when a man's end is upon him, an angel appears on yonder hill and calls for the man whom he will take, and the man hastens to go across to him and never comes back again; we say that he has crossed over the hill.' 'If that be so,' said the man who was afraid of death, 'when the angel comes and calls for me, he can go on calling for as long as you please: I won't budge from where I am.'

So years and seasons passed and the time came for this man too to cross over the hill, that is to say, for him to die. One day, as he was being shaved in the barber's shop, his angel came and called for him; the man was in such a hurry to go that he would not wait for the barber to shave the other side of his face, but ran off and crossed over the hill.

So gentle a thing is death.

[1] Text from Pontos; printed in *Arkheion Pontou*, i. 196.

ADDENDA TO
'MODERN GREEK FOLKTALES'

IT seems convenient to print here a list of the variants of the stories in *M.G.F.* which are not listed in that book. Some of them, indeed, had not then appeared, nor had I sufficiently searched in my old notebooks for what I have transcribed there from the manuscript stories in the collections of the National Lexicon now being compiled at Athens. Nor had I seen the book, published only in 1953, of stories from Symi by Miss Eirini Moskóvi, *Tales from my own Country*, *Παραμύθια τῆς πατρίδας μου*, a good and important collection. Here then are my addenda:

In the manuscripts of the National Lexicon are further variants of the following: of Nos. 3, 19, 21, 38, 56, from Pontos, and of Nos. 31, 32, from Megara.

The following are the variants from Miss Moskóvi's book: No. 14 of *M.G.F.* is Moskóvi, p. 91; No. 20 is M., p. 36; No. 22 is M., p. 110; No. 26 is M., p. 68; No. 29 is M., p. 61; No. 31 is M., p. 116; No. 36 is M., p. 44; No. 44 is M., p. 9; No. 47 is M., p. 16; No. 60 is M., p. 54; No. 69 is M., p. 101; No. 83*b* is M., p. 28.

The other addenda are as follows:

No. 2. THE LITTLE BOY AND HIS ELDER SISTER.
Add: Aitolia, in *Laographía*, ii. 388.

No. 3. THE BOY CALLED THIRTEEN.
Add: Mytilene, in Kretschmer, *Der heutige lesbische Dialekt*, p. 532.

No. 6. THE QUEST FOR THE FAIR ONE OF THE WORLD.
Add: Epeiros, in Pio, *Contes populaires grecs*, No. 16, p. 52.

No. 14. THE GIRL WITH TWO HUSBANDS.
Add: Cf. *Arkheíon Pontou*, vii. 110.

No. 15. THE GIFT TO THE YOUNGEST DAUGHTER.
Add: Pontos, in *Arkheíon Pontou*, xi. 130, and Rhodes, in Vrontis, *Rodiakà Laographikà*, ii. 101.

No. 18. THE ANIMAL WIFE.
Add: Kálymnos, in Dieterich, *Sprache und Volksüberlieferungen der südl. Sporaden*, p. 487; Mykonos, in Roussel, *Contes de Mycone*, No. 3; Naxos, in *Neoellinikà Análekta*, ii. 46.

No. 22. THE MAGIC BIRD.
Add: Chios, in Argenti, *Folklore of Chios*, p. 588.

No. 24. MASTER AND PUPIL.
Add: Mykonos, in Roussel, ibid., Nos. 41, 42; and Pontos, in *Arkheíon Pontou*, vii. 106.

No. 27. THE STRIGLA.
Add: Aitolia, in *Laographía*, ii. 385.

No. 28. THE THREE WONDERFUL DOGS.
Add: Epeiros, in Pio, p. 36.

No. 31. THE THREE SISTERS AND THEIR WISHES FOR A HUSBAND.
Add: Aravan, in Cappadocia, in *Mikrasiatiká Khroniká*, v. 162.

No. 38. THE YOUNGER BROTHER RESCUES THE ELDER.
Add: Thera, in *Deffner's Archiv*, i. 133; in this book No. 6.

No. 39. THE PRINCE IN DISGUISE.
Add: Epeiros, in Pio, p. 6.

No. 47. IS IT A BOY? IS IT A GIRL?
Add: Chios, in Argenti and Rose, *Folklore of Chios*, p. 584.

No. 49. THE STORY OF FIORENDINO.
Add: Thera, in *Parnassós*, ix. 370, a story with several of the points of *Fiorendino*.

No. 50. THE MAN BORN TO BE KING.
Add: Macedonia, in *Laographía*, ii. 589.

No. 51. THE ORDERING OF THE FATES.
Add: Vourlá, near Smyrna, in *Mikrasiatiká Khroniká*, iv. 248, and *Khroniká tou Pontou*, ii. 579.

No. 56. THE THIEF IN THE KING'S TREASURY.
Add: Argenti, *Folklore of Chios*, p. 591.

No. 57. THE GIRL WHO WAS LEFT AT HOME.
Add: Aravan, in Cappadocia, in *Mikrasiatiká Khroniká*, v. 173.

No. 70. ONLY ONE BROTHER WAS GRATEFUL.
Add: Pontos, in *Arkheíon Pontou*, xi. 93; Cyprus, in *Kypriaká Khroniká*, ix. 287; Thrace, in *Thrakiká*, xvii. 183; Macedonia, in *Laographía*, vi. 513; Zákynthos, ibid., x. 429.

No. 72. THE TWO BROTHERS AND THE UMPIRE.
Add: Zákynthos, in *Laographía*, xi. 483.

No. 74. THE WOMAN GRANTED TO SEE THE ANGEL OF DEATH.
Add: Pontos, in *Arkheíon Pontou*, xi. 132.

No. 76. THE TWO WOMEN AND THE TWELVE MONTHS.
Add: Mytilene, in Nikítas, *Tò lesviakó Minológio*, p. 13.

No. 79. THE SEARCH FOR LUCK.
Add: Pontos, in *Arkheíon Pontou*, xi. 90.

No. 80. A JUST MAN FOR A GODFATHER.
Add: Macedonia, in *Laographía*, vi. 508.

No. 83. THE MERCY OF GOD.
Add: Epeiros, in *Sýllogos*, xiv. 258, No. 5.

Index

Alexander romance, 5.
Animal stories, No. 3.
Apollonios of Tyre, 18.
Ashes of a dead man, 34.
Athánatos, 30.

Babies in paradise, 169.
Bets, The two, 78.
Blackamoor, 74.
Blindness cured by herb, 153, 154.
Born of the Moon, No. 14.
Born of the Sun, No. 14.

Christ, in form of a monk, 90.
Corpse-eating woman, 49.
Cupid and Psyche, 18.
Curtain to keep out the day, 46, 52.
Cyclops, No. 4.

Dartané, 60.
Death, crossing over the hill to, 173.
Death and the Old Woman, 172.
Depe Ghoz, 14; *see* Tepekozis.
Douglas, Norman, 119.

Easter, celebrated in Paradise, 164.
Embroidery, 129, 134.
Epilepsy, 44.
Erysichthon, 17.
Eyes, blue or dark, 94, 100.

Fates of men, 113.
Father and Son, 30, 155, 162.
Fisherman, 97.
Flute played to snake, 77, 79, 81.

St. George, No. 25.
Gesture language, 10.
Giustiniani, *History of Chios*, 18.
Good sense, 118.
Gourd hung up to rattle, 40.

Horse, incarnating blessing of parents, 61.

Immortality, Water of, 5.
Italian names, 56.

Jew, 80, 126.
Jinn of the Sea, 68.

King of the Sea, 132.
Knife, Rope, Stone, No. 5.

Lamia, 64.
Lamps of men's lives, 113.
Local names, 123.
Luck, No. 19, No. 20.

Mass said for the dead, 160.
Medea, 17.
Meleager, 16.
Mirror of Princes, 155.
Mountains clashing together, 84.

Next World, accounts of, 164.
No Man, No. 4.
Novels, 137, 155.

Oghuz, 14.
Ogress, 64.

Pairs, Men created in pairs, 153.
Parody of a story, No. 17.
Pastures of the Sun, 138, 146, 151.
Pipe, making a castle move, 67.
Plane tree rooted in a man's ear, 106.
Pleiad, 1.
Polly the Fox, 10.
Polykrates, 119.
Polyphemos, No. 4.
Priest ignorant of the service, 87.
Pursuit, magical pursuit and escape, 1.

Ring, lost, 122.
Root of a tree hiding treasure, 150.

Sandy Batoum, No. 2.
Schlirionte, 18.
Snake in a woman's body, 106.

Snake dancing to a flute, 81.
Star of Dawn, 1.
Strigla, 46, 48.
Sun invoked to give help, 82.
Sun, his mother, 84.
Sword laid in bed, 30.

Tepekózis, Cyclops, 14.
Three-eyed ghoul, 129.
Tongues of monsters cut out, 123.
Tsakonian, 130.
Twelve Councillors, 162.
'Twoness' in things created, 155.

Vatka village, 130.
Versification in stories, 55.

Weapon, choosing a rusty weapon, 30, 36.
White Sea, 121.
Wild man, No. 7.
World Below, 71.

www.ingramcontent.com/pod-product-compliance
Lightning Source LLC
Chambersburg PA
CBHW060528310726
48982CB00002B/471

* 9 7 8 0 8 3 7 1 7 6 3 1 4 *